DANGER IN THE DEUX SEVRES

Catherine Patterson Mysteries

GM HALEY

No part of this book may be produced by any means, nor transmitted, nor translated into a machine language without the written permission of the author

BOOKS IN THIS SERIES

DANGER IN THE DEUX SEVRES

VENGEANCE IN THE VENDEE

CHICANERY IN THE CHARENTE

For Norma H
Mother and Friend
Forever in my heart

PROLOGUE

She sat facing the door. In her lucid moments, she held onto some tiny vestige of hope that her rescuer would at any moment come through it.

Her head lolled once again toward her chest. Fighting to stay conscious only made her more aware of her situation: wrists and ankles tightly bound and sore; throat hoarse and dry; her head and back aching from being forced to sit upright for so long on the hard wooden chair.

"Yousef" she croaked, her voice little more than a whisper.

"*...contact*" A voice boomed in front of her as she tried vainly to look up at her captor. Her vision blurred as she looked through the slits in the swollen skin of her eyes, seeing only the shape. The bulk. The stench. The malevolence of the beast before her.

Pain suddenly seared the skin on her cheek as once again, a sharp slap forced her momentarily into wakefulness.

"*No one is coming for you!...Your contact*"

The voice, as if from far away, as if from a loud speaker, an echo almost, assaulted her sanity. The words made no sense. Sudden nausea took hold and she retched. Her body jerked in an attempt to lurch forward causing the restraints to dig painfully into her waist and wrists.

Then – a sudden gust of fresh clean air blasted across her face. In desperation, she struggled to suck in the air, endeavouring to cleanse her lungs of the stale, stuffy, filth of her tiny prison cell.

Sensing, rather than seeing someone else in the room, she braced herself for further pain. But then she *felt*, rather than sensed, the hard, coarseness of twisted fibres pushed roughly over her head and placed around her neck. She *felt*, rather than sensed, her body being lifted roughly. *Felt* the constriction around her throat as she made one last tiny effort in her exhausted state to fight for life. And then finally, *felt* herself succumb to calmness and serenity as her life slipped away.

CHAPTER ONE

Wednesday

The roads were quiet. Nothing unusual in that. Rural France often seemed deserted. As if the zombie apocalypse had already taken place and I was the only one left alive searching for survivors and trying to avoid an attack of flesh eating ghouls.While pondering the inadvertent benefits of total annihilation I checked the clock on the dash before dismissing this flight of fancy. Eleven twenty – *what was I thinking?* It was far too close to midday to see evidence of civilisation. Preparations for lunch would be in full swing. Fine cuisine would soon be in the process of being savoured by self appointed gourmands who would deliberate the chef's ingenuity (or lack of it) as well as choice of ingredients and flavours. Perhaps on the return journey I'd spot some sign of life, though I couldn't bet on it. Before lunch had time to settle, it was likely that dinner arrangements would be in operation. I smiled at the thought of how French daily life was taken over by the passion for food and yet somehow this same foible endeared me to their national character.Suddenly realising that I'd driven further than expected and had no memory of familiar parts of the road, I sighed loudly and forced myself to remain focused. Taking note instead of the surroundings, I was surprised at how much foliage there was for the time of year. The warmth in the air over the past week had brought the spring flowers into bloom and they now sat in their full glory bordering the road and interspersed among the hedges. Occasionally along the route, tiny pink and white petals floated down on the breeze from trees heavy with blossom.

Feeling uplifted by such beautiful spring weather, I began to reflect on how there had been a considerable boost in my mood over the last few days. Not that I was usually miserable, but I was given to bouts of melancholy and had recently convinced myself that the lack of sunlight was an attributing factor. Certain that I was among the multitude of people who endured low moods due to sunlight deficiency, the idea of buying an artificial sun lamp to recreate the light needed sat at the back of my mind. Did they work? There was bound to be myriad reviews on the vendors' websites but then sitting around waiting to see if an artificial light was working didn't seem to be time well spent. And then what if an improved mood was merely a result of the power of suggestion?

Catching sight of the sign up ahead which said '*Creperie*' brought my internal monologue to an end.

Indicating right at the junction I pulled the car off the main road and steered it down a steep, narrow bank, flanked on both sides by tall, leafy trees and bushes. After about a hundred yards or so I came to the tiny parking area behind the restaurant. My heart sank when I observed around half a dozen cars parked there already, including Di's four wheel drive which easily dwarfed the others. Reversing was not one of my strong points and I cursed repeatedly as I struggled to fit the car into a tight spot in between.

Finally, after some to-ing and fro-ing, I left the car to walk around the building to the front of the restaurant. I could feel the warmth from the sun on my face and even though it was just mid- morning, I marveled once again at such pleasing weather for early spring; perhaps it was the sign of a great summer to come.

I scanned the seated area on my approach and observed Di looking firmly settled at a table on the terrace. On spotting me her face lit up with a smile and she lifted her hand in greeting. I returned the wave while lauding her achievement at managing to gain an enviable spot. Her table was situated within just a few feet of a dry stone wall; a wall that dropped down quite dramatically on the other side to a grassy verge surrounding a large lake. It was a lofty position which would provide us with a magnificent view of our surroundings including the vast expanse of the lake which at that moment was dancing with tiny white lights due to the sun bouncing off its surface. A small island sat in the centre of the lake with a great cluster of trees standing tall and proud. These provided a much needed canopy of shelter for the array of swans and ducks which lived there.

However, it was the view beyond the vegetation which was a sight to behold and one which could not fail to inspire limitless wonder. As if raised up from the lake itself were the medieval ramparts of a chateau with stone walls seeming to stretch majestically skyward. Despite being acquainted with the knowledge that the lake was originally manmade, this magnificent view still brought to mind my personal image of Avalon. Arthurian legend was what I liked to call my 'chosen specialized subject' after absorbing copious amount of books on the topic and I'd developed a clear picture in my mind. As a result, each time I visited this restaurant I almost expected an arm to suddenly emerge from beneath the depths with the mighty sword Excalibur clutched in its hand. The thought was a fruitless exercise in self delusion as I knew I'd be forever disappointed.

While my imagination ran wild, I picked my way between the tables and headed toward Di. We hugged warmly before sitting, but didn't greet in the 'french style' of kissing on both cheeks. It was a custom I was grateful we hadn't succumbed to as I always felt like a fraud – as if I were pretending to be French when it was so obvious I wasn't. Di could probably get away with it though, she'd been living in France for over six years and spoke significantly better French than I could ever hope to.

Diane Harley, 'Di' for short was a dear friend I had known for more than twenty years. She'd been the one to spur me into action of making the break from Blighty and taking a step into the unknown. This 'get together' was our monthly chat to catch up. Sometimes we'd visit each other at home, other times we'd head to a favourite spot to enjoy the food and character of the place. On those occasions we tried to make a habit of meeting somewhere equidistant from where we both lived so it was fairer than one of us having to travel a longer distance. Today we'd each had only a twenty minute trip with Di journeying from her village near the

Atlantic coast and me coming from the opposite direction further inland.

Due to the unseasonably warm weather Di was wearing a summery short sleeved blue cotton dress. A darker blue, silken scarf was draped loosely around her shoulders. It was a different look for her. She had also changed her hair colour. A natural brunette, she was now blonde. It looked natural because she was fair skinned and I commented on how well it suited her.

She pulled a face in response and pushed back a strand of unruly hair. "Well unfortunately, there were too many grey hairs to contend with so I decided they'd be easier to hide this way."

"Mm, know what you mean", I nodded in agreement while thinking of my own attempts to conceal the signs of advancing age. Not that we were old. Forty something is *definitely* not old.

"And that's a beautiful scarf you're wearing...is it silk?

"Yeah...did you notice the sequins?" She held up both ends of the scarf to show off the fine detail of the embroidery and tiny sparkling sequins which embellished the edges.

"Phil brought it back from his last trip. It was given as a gift *for his wife* from his interpreter..."

"That was nice of him." I acknowledged nodding.

Di looked amused.

"*Her!*"

I mouthed a silent *Oh* and looked at her expectantly, waiting for more information.

She didn't disappoint.

"Apparently...she was leaving the area and as she practically works for the company full time...and for Phil in particular..."

I nodded but said nothing, just waiting for more.

"*And* she wears the full burqha..." She added, laughing softly as if guessing my thoughts.

"No worries there then!" I grinned wryly. Though I fully accepted her belief that there was no reason to suspect anything other than a working relationship. I certainly hadn't been made aware of any past infidelities Phil had been involved in. But, hey, what did I know?

Deciding to change the subject, I pulled my chair closer to the table as I glanced casually around to gauge how busy the place was. Nearby was a table of three elderly men chatting, wine already on the table. At another table sat a young couple drinking espressos and studying the menu in great detail. A third table was taken up by a man who was sitting alone, his face obscured by the newspaper he was reading. A family with two young children were just making their way to the inside of the restaurant.

I turned back to Di.

"Well it doesn't look too busy. Getting served shouldn't be a bother."

Sure enough the waiter was there just seconds later. Di ordered our *grand crèmes* and we settled down to our chat.

Our conversation usually followed a sort of routine. First we focused on our respective families. Everything was brought up to date. Di's husband Phil worked in Libya as an engineer. She told me he wasn't due to return home for about three weeks since he'd just gone back after his month off. I was never quite sure exactly what his job entailed but he had some sort of supervisory engineering position related to drilling for oil. I then got the latest on their daughter, Emma. A junior designer, Emma was by all accounts making quite a name for herself in one of the French fashion houses based in Paris. Di bristled with pride as she passed on descriptions of the 'fashion' events in Emma's life. I was suitably impressed and made all the appropriate 'wowing' noises. I then waited just long enough to be sure she was finished her news before bringing her up to date with mine.

I reminded her about Karl's meeting. Karl was my husband who had travelled to London a few days earlier to complete some legal papers for the publishers he worked for. They had insisted he needed to be present to witness his signature, so he was staying over for a couple of days and was due to fly back at the end of the week. Having left his full time job as a graphic artist when we had moved to France, Karl had been fulfilling his lifetime dream of working as an illustrator. A children's publisher had got wind of how good he was from some connections with a former colleague and he'd then been offered some casual work which meant he had the freedom to work from home.   When he didn't have a 'project' to work on, he was kept busy on another of his passions, renovating an old outbuilding. We had acquired two of them with our land.

"Is Chloe still in Beijing?"

I nodded "Spoke to her on Skype …just last night actually."

Chloe was our daughter. Currently in Beijing with her boyfriend, Chris. She was working as a travel writer. Although she was paid as a regular journalist she often supplemented her salary with the odd bit of freelance writing which she frequently sold to various newspapers and magazines. It gave her the opportunity to travel and she often got to stay in some of the world's swankiest hotels.   Chris also worked freelance as a photographer so he could afford the time to travel with her while she was working.

I continued. "She said she was allowed a couple of weeks for the assignment even though it would only take her about four days to complete.   They're thinking about going further into the country - get some experience of the real China, she said."

"Sounds great! I wish I'd been able to go off on adventures like that when I was young...cos that's the time to do it...So anyway, how's Aidan doing?"

I reminded her that Aidan, our son, was coming up to his final exams in history and archaeology. He was studying at York University in England.

"Did I tell you about his plan to travel around Australia after his finals with a group of friends? They want to stay there for about four months."

Di nodded, acknowledging that she already knew some of the details.

"Well, he's announced he'll be backpacking - He said staying in hostels would keep the cost down...I've met the friends he's going to be travelling with and they seem a good bunch so I think he'll be okay..." My voice trailed off.

Di interrupted. " Oh, loads of them do it - he'll be fine!" she said dismissively, flicking her hand as if to shoo away any worries I might have.

Just then our coffees arrived so we paused long enough for the waiter to leave us before continuing.

"Mmm...Well after that he'll be coming to France - around the end of September. It'll be good to see him."

I fell silent then, folding a napkin absent mindedly while my thoughts were taken up with Aidan. I hadn't seen him since Christmas and was really looking forward to his visit. I was also hoping he might decide to stay in France - at least for a little while.

"Yes." Di sighed suddenly and stared sullenly into her coffee cup. "It's nice when they return home."

Aware that our moods were becoming sombre and it was probably my fault, I shook myself out of the reverie and changed tack.

Forcing a smile I said breezily. "So...how about you? Did you go to that exhibition you mentioned?"

"Yes" she looked up and smiled, appearing glad to change the subject. "*And*...I have been asked if I would like to display my art work!"

"Fantastic!"

A couple of weeks ago, Di had gone into a newly opened art exhibition room in her local village to have a look around the paintings. The owner, a woman Di described as 'Bohemian', had discovered through chatting, that Di was also an artist and had asked her to bring in a couple of her 'pieces'. On seeing them she had enthused over the work and asked if she could put them on display. She'd suggested that Di would only have to contribute a small fee for each painting sold. No sale, no fee.

"So there's nothing to lose and it's a great opportunity to get my work seen." She paused, considering, "and even if I don't sell any at least it'll get rid of some of the stack at home".

"I'm sure you'll sell something," I said encouragingly. "Your work is really good." And I meant it. I already owned a couple of her paintings. One of Chloe, where she'd taken the likeness from a photograph of when she was very young. Another was of a forest clearing with faeries hidden amongst the undergrowth. It was unusual but charming and always drew admiring comments from visitors to the house.

Di changed the subject.

"How long have you got till your reporter turns up?"

The reporter she was referring to was a columnist from the magazine 'Enjoy France' who was coming to interview me. The magazine wanted to run an article about our chambres d'hôtes. After having had three successful years so far running the place with my husband, we were now going to get free publicity from a magazine for Francophiles.

"She said she'd get into the area about three. Apparently she's got a sat' nav' so said that finding the place shouldn't be a problem."

"Famous last words" mused Di looking at her watch. "Well, we've got plenty of time. Let's get a bite to eat."

I agreed wholeheartedly as we picked up the menus simultaneously and began to scan the array of *crêpes* and *galettes* offered by the chef. We managed to order our *galettes* filled with ham and cheese fairly quickly as the waiter was hovering nearby and we both chose to finish off with another coffee. While eating we talked about the guests I had staying with us. I usually gave Di a rundown of what I perceived them to be like because I often didn't get to know them too well – especially if they'd only stayed over for one or two nights. Sometimes I would get to know a little about the family who were renting the gîte. It just depended if they were around when I was. I tried not to bother them and just let them enjoy their holiday.

As two fifteen approached we decided it was time to move. Apart from needing to leave for my appointment, we were worried the owners of the restaurant might think we'd taken up residence.

I was trying to get the waiter's attention for the bill when Di's phone rang.

"*L'addition, s'il vous plaît.*" I said after finally catching his eye.

Turning back to the table Di was finishing her phone call.

"That was short and sweet."

Di looked bemused.

"It was the woman from the exhibition room. Said she's got an offer from someone I can't possibly refuse. She wanted to know if I could get there by three thirty to meet someone." She looked at her watch, then at me expectantly.

"What d'you think?"

I shrugged. "Sounds intriguing."

"It does, doesn't it?" She looked again at her watch. "The thing is I'd have to leave sharp to get there in time." She pulled a face.

"Well then you'd better get going!" I ordered lightheartedly. "I'll sort out the bill, it's my shout anyway."

"Oh thanks!"

Looking grateful and not needing further persuasion, she hastily picked up her bag and made her way around the table. After giving me a quick peck on the cheek she was off.

"I'll ring to let you know all about it!" She called over her shoulder as if on an afterthought.

"See that you do!" I shouted amicably in reply.

Having settled the bill I got up to leave the table, noticing just by chance that Di's scarf, which had slid from her shoulders earlier, had been left forgotten on her seat. Deciding she wasn't in desperate need of it, I pushed it casually into my bag, resolving to pass it on to her next time we met.

Strolling slowly toward the car park, I was conscious of someone following directly behind. Slowing down a little while rummaging in my bag for car keys, I moved to the side to let whoever it was pass. At that moment a couple of young children darted out in front of me so I stopped dead to ensure I didn't tread on them. As the children's parents were following closely, I hung back to let them pass. Once they were well in front, I continued toward the car, keys now firmly in hand.

Instinctively feeling there was still someone else behind me, I glanced quickly around before opening the car door. Seeing there was noone there, I decided my mind was simply playing tricks. All the same, once seated in the car I felt the urge to check the rear view mirror. As I turned the key to start the engine I caught sight of a man standing at the edge of the car park, his back toward the car as he looked out across the lake. He was enjoying a cigarette. Concluding he must have been the person I'd sensed had followed me out of the restaurant yet was clearly someone who was just being considerate enough to smoke away from the other diners, I breathed an inward sigh of relief. I wasn't losing it after all. Pressing down on the accelerator I pulled out of the car park without giving it further thought.

*

On the way home I did a quick detour to the supermarket to get a few bits and pieces yet still managed to arrive back at the house with ten minutes to spare.

On approaching the house I saw my neighbour, Sue, pushing a wheel barrow across the lane from the house toward her garden and waved in greeting. She responded with a smile and a nod rather than releasing her gloved hands from the handles and carried on with her work.

Sue was a divorcée who had been living in our little hamlet for about two years. She had four horses which she kept in stables behind her house and was attempting to set up a riding school - though wading through French bureaucracy to get her English qualifications recognized was causing her some consternation.

Entering the hallway I noticed a faint musky smell and it occurred to me that someone else had been there. That was okay. The outside door was deliberately left unlocked because guests were encouraged to leave messages for me there if I wasn't around. I couldn't see any messages had been left but noticed the reservation book was still on the table top. If my memory served me right, I'd taken the book out of the drawer to check the time of the appointment, scanned down the page of names and phone numbers but then replaced it before I'd left for the restaurant. Yet strangely the book wasn't in its designated place. Frowning, I reflected on the downside of advancing age and sighed deeply but decided it didn't really matter in the big scheme of things. The book was only meant as a backup hard copy anyway. I kept important details of guests on the computer. The book just made it easier to get a quick look at reservations rather than wait for the computer to start up.

I unlocked the hallway door into the house. This was our area. The house was a large converted barn with a large open plan kitchen and living room. Stairs to the right of the door led up to two bedrooms and one bathroom. Opposite was a third, larger bedroom with ensuite bathroom. We had renovated the barn ourselves about ten years earlier. It was originally a large building in two parts but one of those parts was in such disrepair that it had to be demolished. On considering the move to France we had decided to invest in rebuilding the section which had been demolished. This new area of our home was now used as the *chambres d'hôtes.* Guests had a choice of three upstairs bedrooms, all with en suite bathrooms. The ground floor area was used as a dining area for breakfast and a small lounge where I kept an array of local magazines, maps and leaflets giving information about the region. The chambres d'hôtes had separate access from the courtyard at the back and large french windows were set into the wall at the front of the lounge. There was also an adjoining door from the lounge into our kitchen which was kept locked after I cleared away breakfast dishes each morning. The view from the french windows from both our house and the chambres d'hôtes was of the landscaped garden. This was, I thought, one of the main attractions of staying as a guest. Each year, as winter morphed into spring, the garden would burst into life and stay lush and green right through till the end of October. The borders, once in bloom were intensely vivid with colour. An orchard planted over to the right of the garden a few years earlier was now producing olives, plums, apples and pears. A heated, rectangular swimming pool, was sited over to the left and surrounded by huge boulders and conifers, acting as a barrier for safety as required by French law. In the centre toward the end of the garden, there was an elegant stone sculpture of a water nymph, which drew the eye toward the view of the rolling countryside and hills beyond. These were the Gatîne hills in the heart of the Deux Sevres. It was such a beautiful view and I never tired of looking at it.

I took a few moments to look around the house. Wanting to double check everything was in place. Maybe the reporter would take photographs? I had already decided we would sit on the terrace just outside the french windows for the interview as I wanted to show off the view. It was a south facing garden and the heat and glare generated by the sun could be unbearable so the tiled portico above the terrace provided much needed shade. A large rustic table which could seat at least a dozen people and was used frequently for outside dining, especially in the summer months, took up a fair amount of space on the terrace. It had already been laid with a few items of crockery together with a vase of fresh flowers which I hoped wouldn't attract too many insects, (the bees having already discovered the new lilac coloured blossoms on the bougainvillea which was draped loosely around the columns supporting the portico).

To keep occupied while I was waiting, I decided to water some of the plants. Brightly coloured geraniums were lined up in pots of varying sizes and colours near the front entrance and were, due to the warm weather, becoming increasingly desperate for a drink. It was on my second visit to the water butt when I heard the sound of a car engine as it came into the hamlet. To satisfy my curiosity I headed toward the courtyard, watering can still in hand. A small red Renault pulled to a halt and an attractive young woman, petite in stature with olive skin and long brown hair stepped out of the car. She wasn't much older than Chloe I thought, perhaps about twenty six. She smiled in greeting and guessing she was the much awaited reporter I returned her smile and offered her my free hand.

"Miss Shakil I presume?"

"Yes, hello, Sophie please." She quickly turned to slam the car door shut before taking my hand. I noticed the colour of her eyes were grey – unusual given her complexion.

"You must be Catherine."

She had such a friendly demeanour I warmed to her immediately.

"That's right. Did you fly down?" I asked noticing the car was a left hand drive with french plates so presumably a hire car.

Heading toward the back of the car to open the boot she called over her shoulder.

"Yes, I drove to Southampton then caught a flight to La Rochelle."

She pulled out a medium sized holdall, which I estimated was just about the right size for the four night stay and I gestured toward the entrance of the chambres d'hôtes.

"I'm assuming you'd like to freshen up before doing anything else so I'll show you your room straightaway."

"Oh lovely." She beamed as she glanced briefly around at her surroundings.

I led her upstairs to her room while we chatted about the unseasonally warm weather. She said it had also been warm in England so she'd packed some light summer clothes just in case.

Wanting to impress, I had given her the room at the front which looked out onto the garden. It was decorated in pale green shades with modern pine furniture and it had the best view. It didn't disappoint. As soon as Sophie got through the door, she put down her bags and made her way to the window, expressing delight at such beautiful scenery. Finally, she did a quick appraisal of the room's interior.

"It's gorgeous!"

"Glad you like it" I smiled, feeling very pleased with myself.

We arranged to meet downstairs on the terrace about twenty minutes later and I left her to unpack.

I had just brewed a fresh pot of coffee and put some bite sized pastries on the table when Sophie appeared. She had changed her clothes into a simple yellow shift dress and looked altogether more relaxed. I saw her look keenly toward the coffee pot and beckoned her to take a seat.

"I have tea if you'd prefer" I offered.

"No, no the coffee smells delicious."

She sank down onto a seat with a wistful sigh and I poured out the coffee. Looking around at the view she commented on how lucky we were and I saw her gazing longingly toward the pool.

"Feel free to use the pool while you're here, it's certainly warm enough." I pushed the plate full of bite sized pastries a little in her direction.

"We have a gîte, as you know," I continued, "and the families renting it know that it's shared with the chambres d'hôtes' guests so there's no problem."

"Oh I might take you up on that as it looks so inviting in this weather." She took a sip of coffee from her cup and helped herself to a pastry, studying it absent mindedly before replying.

"We've certainly had some rave reviews about this place in letters to the magazine, as you know, which is why we're so interested in writing the article about it. It's one of those uplifting success stories of expats which our readers like so much. And on first impressions I can see why we have such great reports."

I was pleased at such positive feedback and glad that all the hard work had paid off. Although my husband and I were a great team, he left me to run the business. I kept the website updated, took bookings, looked after the guests at breakfast and made sure rooms were clean and ready for new arrivals. Karl was always on hand to undertake any repairs or sort out any practical issues I wasn't able to deal with. This was *exactly* how I liked it.

I asked Sophie about herself. She told me that she used to be involved in investigative journalism and had spent some time abroad doing that but didn't seem keen to elaborate further. She explained that she had worked for the magazine for just over a year and enjoyed what she called the 'light heartedness' of it. She also rented a flat in London and was saving to put a deposit down on one she could own. It was, she said, proving difficult with property prices constantly rising. She referred in passing to her family; an English mother and Egyptian father.

Our conversation was interrupted by the phone ringing so I excused myself and went to answer it. It was Karl. He said that he was going to stay in London over the coming weekend because he'd arranged to meet Aidan. They'd found out about a comic convention at Earl's Court and wanted to attend. He would therefore be home later than he originally intended and he was going to book a flight for Monday instead. I told him the reporter had arrived and he wished me luck on making a good impression.

Putting the receiver down, I noticed the message received button was flashing so decided to quickly check the messages. There were two - both cancellations for guests due to arrive at the chambres d'hôtes on Thursday, the following day. I felt instantly disappointed and breathed a heavy sigh. I had been so looking forward to having the place full of guests this week. I'd wanted to put the chambres d'hôtes in the best possible light, keen as I was to make everything look good for the reporter. Unfortunately the messages only served to remind me that potential guests had the right to cancel on a whim and I was powerless to do anything about it. Feeling that I needed to make a hasty return to the one important guest I actually had, I resolved to put it from my mind. This was easier said than done. On the return to the terrace, involuntary thoughts filled my mind about the hurried manner in which the messages were left with no reasons given.

Despite best intentions, I must have been frowning.

"Problem?"

Sophie had known me for such a short time yet had a look of genuine concern on her face.

"No, no, nothing important really." I forced a smile while trying to keep any trace of frustration from my tone.

"Would you like a tour of the place?" I asked, deliberately upbeat.

"Great. I'd love a tour!" Sophie responded cheerfully before quickly draining the vestiges of coffee from what was her second cup and stood up, brushing a few invisible crumbs from her dress.

I motioned towards the garden and we left the terrace. She fell into step alongside as I veered automatically to the left, drawn toward the herbaceous border. She pulled ahead a little, attracted no doubt by the bright yellow blossoms of the Forsythia which were delicately interspersed with fresh lime green bracts of a

Euphorbia. With thoughts of her magazine article and feeling buoyed by her cheerful demeanour, I gave Sophie the benefit of some horticultural knowledge as we strolled, keen to impart information about the variety of plants and shrubs planted with the aim of softening the hard landscaping of the garden.

Only minutes into the floral instruction, there came a great grunting engine sound from the lane behind the house. Curiosity got the better of me.

"Sounds like we've got company" I said as I cut short the tour and led Sophie in the direction of the lane instead.

A huge red fire engine was pulling up outside Lesley and Tim's, our neighbours' house, opposite just as Lesley came scurrying towards us looking flustered.

"Hello Catherine!" She grimaced and glanced briefly at Sophie in greeting.

I'd been so caught up in ensuring the house looked good, I hadn't even noticed Lesley and Tim had arrived. They usually lived in Scotland during the winter months and came to stay at their holiday home in France, from spring till autumn.

On entering the house, Lesley explained, she and Tim had found the cellar flooded and the floor tiles lifting in the kitchen. Having sought advice from Monsieur Sabiron, the old farmer next door, he had suggested asking the *sapeur pompiers* to pump out the water.

"We think it's the sheer amount of rain that you've had here over the winter," she gushed. "Because of the slope in the garden at the back of the house, the rain hasn't had time to seep into the soil and has leaked into the house." She pulled a face and sighed. "I suppose it doesn't help having a '*cave*' underneath," she added shaking her head glumly.

"Oh dear." I said trying to sound sympathetic "Weren't you storing wine down there in the cellar?" Which if I remembered rightly had been very expensive.

She nodded, looking thoroughly fed up.

"Maybe the wine will still be ok, once everything's cleaned up." She looked at me and Sophie hopefully.

"*Allez!*"

There were three firefighters shouting instructions to each other, one driving the fire engine and the other two pulling at some sort of hose which snaked its way into Lesley's house. We watched their comings and goings for a while as if transfixed. Finally, the driver began reversing the fire engine just as our attention was diverted toward a tall, dark and ruggedly handsome young fireman who came sauntering toward us; his short sleeves showing his already tanned, sinewy arms.

"*Eets* ok now," he stopped to address Lesley, towering over her as he searched for the right words.

She looked at him open mouthed. Perhaps it wasn't just me admiring him.

"'eet needs to dry out...er..." He gave a Gallic shrug. " Per'aps to stop the smell of the damp but eets ok now." He grinned suddenly and I noticed his sidelong glance at Sophie.

Lesley gave him a winning smile.

"Thank you so much!"

She turned to me. "André, it turns out, is the mayor's son."

"Oh!"

I studied André for a moment until it dawned on me how alike they were. The mayor (or *maire*, to give him his french title) his father, was an amicable anglophile who had become a regular visitor to our hamlet. Though he could easily send someone less important, he often turned up himself with official documents. These usually related to some sort of legal permission for renovations or alterations on houses in the hamlet. He was usually eager to chat, practise his English and of course have a glass of wine or two.

I smiled at André in recognition and noticing his reluctance to leave, introduced Sophie, saying simply that she was a guest staying with us. Sophie, I noted, looked rather flushed. She responded to the introduction by giving André a rather coy smile but said nothing. He in turn, appeared suddenly shy and merely nodded in her direction mumbling "*mademoiselle*". Aware of this awkward interaction, Lesley and I briefly exchanged amused glances before André turned back toward the fire engine. The three of us then watched in admiration as André grabbed hold of the huge door to the front cabin of the fire engine and hauled himself up into the seat next to the driver. He slammed the door shut and rested his arm on the ledge of the open window. Very smoothly done I thought. Glancing briefly in our direction and with a slight wave of the hand he shouted.

"*A bientôt!*"

As the driver turned the fire engine to move off down the lane, I saw André's gaze return to linger momentarily on Sophie.

CHAPTER TWO

Lesley took a deep breath and looked toward the house.

"Well, I suppose I'd better go and survey the damage." She hesitated, turning to look at me and Sophie. "Do you want to come and have a look? I need some moral support. Tim's just popped to the supermarket for provisions before the cleanup starts," she added, as if to explain why she was alone.

"Yes, of course, and you know, if you need any help, just ask."

I turned to Sophie who was smiling absently.

"Do you...?" I didn't finish.

"Yes, why not" she replied, *still* smiling.

I looked at Lesley to gauge her reaction but her thoughts were now preoccupied.

Lesley led us toward the house and through the main door which opened straight into the kitchen. I surveyed the floor tiles for damage while she took out a torch from one of the drawers.

"We have electricity down there but we're not using it till an electrician's had a look at it. We don't want to go up in a blue light!" She explained while flicking the torch on and off to check it worked.

"No, no, of course not," I grimaced suddenly feeling very sorry for her and Tim. To arrive for a holiday and find there's a flood to deal with couldn't be much fun.

Lesley motioned toward the cellar door and pulled it open. She took the lead while I approached the top step behind her. The air cooled immediately and I gave an involuntary shiver while a rather unpleasant smell of stagnant pond water came to greet us.

"Uh, dear God!" exclaimed Lesley, recoiling slightly.

Sophie and I exchanged glances, our faces showing our disgust. I resolved to try and breathe through my mouth rather than my nose in an effort not to gag. With fingers pinching my nostrils to stifle the smell, I followed Lesley and Sophie stayed closely behind me. All three of us felt for the metal hand rail attached to the wall. It was wet, rusty and covered in silt but it felt sturdy enough to provide a safety grip. Carefully we felt for each step on the narrow stone staircase as gradually our eyes began to adjust to the gloom. On reaching the cellar floor I could make out a long rectangular room, wine racks stood along one side. Some wine bottles still lay untouched in the rack but there were a few smashed on the ground.

"Watch where you put your feet." I warned Sophie who was still hovering behind. "There's some broken glass."

"Well I suppose it could've been worse" said Lesley, shining the light around the room until it settled on a wine rack. "At least some of the wine is still safe, although everything needs rinsing."

An understatement I thought but said nothing. Sophie stumbled and I put my hand out to steady her.

"Thanks" she said gratefully.

Cool air wafted around my ankles.

"Do you feel a draught from somewhere down here?" Sophie voiced my thoughts as she stooped slightly and put out a hand in front of her to feel for the draught. We both looked down the wall to the right of the wine racks.

Lesley swung the torch around the walls randomly.

"There!" I said, copying Sophie's hand actions. Lesley glanced at me to check the direction of my gaze before directing the light.

"Yes...is that a hole?" Lesley moved towards it and put her hand onto the wall. She began to pull at the clumps of soil at the edge of a small opening. It fell away easily.

The air was becoming so cold I could see my breath and I hugged myself to keep out the chill.

Lesley shone the torch into what was now a much larger hole, just about big enough for a small child to climb through. The three of us huddled together to keep out the chill as we peered through. We could see that the ground fell away on the other side in a downward path. The walls looked like they had been purposely hollowed out with what looked like wooden beams embedded into them to give them strength.

We gasped simultaneously.

"It looks like a tunnel" said Sophie.

"Will it go under the house do you think?" I was trying to figure out which direction we were standing in.

Lesley went to pull away at more of the wall but I advised caution.

"It might not be safe." I touched her arm and she stopped, hesitating. "If this tunnel was flooded as well, it could be ready to collapse."

"We could be in danger now," warned Sophie glancing nervously up at the ceiling. "And in fact, I'm feeling a little claustrophobic so think I'll head back up to daylight, and heat."

"That's a good idea." I looked at Lesley "Maybe we should all go back up. You could get in touch with the *geometre* and he could check this all out for you."

"Yes, I might do that" Lesley nodded in agreement.

It was a relief to be back in the daylight even though it was now late in the afternoon and the light was fading. The air outside was becoming cool but it still felt warm after the dankness of the cellar. Lesley thanked us for the offer of help and said that she was going to get started on mopping up in the kitchen. She said she'd get in touch with the *geometre* the following morning to seek advice.

We left Lesley to get on with her cleaning and headed back toward the house. I turned to Sophie.

"Why not catch the last of the sun's rays by spending some time in the garden?" I suggested. "You could familiarise yourself with your surroundings while I prepare an evening meal."

"Yes, I'd like that" she replied. "In fact, I think I'll go and sit by the pool for a while."

"Okay. I'll see you later."

She headed off to the garden and I went into the kitchen. I prepared a simple pasta dish which we ended up sharing around seven. While enjoying a glass of white wine with our dinner, Sophie asked about the name of the chambres d'hôtes.

"*La Chantarelle*. It's a mushroom, I believe?"

"Yes." I laughed softly, a little embarrassed. "I chose the name for the simple reason that I liked the sound of it. Anyway you know how the French like their fungi so I thought it might draw in the crowds."

Sophie smiled and nodded, seemingly satisfied with my reasoning. She began to quiz me about who lived round about in the hamlet. I told her about the house right at the end being occupied by Sue who kept horses and had a large paddock behind her house – the amount of land she had behind the house not being obvious from the front road. I explained that Sue was a school teacher from England who had taken early retirement and moved to France to start up her own riding stables but was currently battling with French bureacracy.

"Once she gets it up and running, it'll be good for our business as well because we can say horse riding is available close by when we advertise."

"Yes, it would certainly be a plus," she agreed. "Especially for people with families in the gîte because it's something to keep children occupied."

I explained that the fourth and final house in the hamlet belonged to an old farmer and his wife,

Monsieur and Madame Sabiron. They lived next door to Lesley and Tim. We had bought the barn from the farmer several years ago and he had long since retired. He and his wife rarely left the vicinity of the hamlet. The only other building apart from the chambres d'hôtes was the gîte. We had a family renting that at the moment. They were due to leave at the weekend.

Eventually our conversation turned to musing about what the tunnel under Lesley's house could have been used for letting our imaginations run wild as we guessed at some sort of smuggling operation or clandestine meetings. Finally, both feeling exhausted, we decided to call it a night.

Sophie left and although I felt weary, I went to check our website in the hope of requests for reservations. Disappointed, I went to bed.

CHAPTER THREE

Thursday

I was awoken abruptly at six thirty by the sound of the phone ringing. In an effort to halt the shrill noise from continuing, I fumbled for the receiver, cursing as I wrestled with it on its way to the floor. Hanging over the edge of the bed I finally managed to put it to my ear and heard Di's voice. She sounded distressed. Anxious to discover the reason why, I pulled myself up to a seated position and rubbed at my eyes, trying to put all my focus into what she was saying. I caught some garbled information about Phil being arrested in Libya.

"*What?*" surely I had misheard.

She was obviously in tears and struggled to explain while she was sobbing and her voice trembling.

"A man from the British consulate in Tripoli telephoned about twenty minutes ago. He said that Phil was taken to a police station. He wasn't sure what it was about and would be in touch as soon as he found anything out."

"But that's a bit out the blue, isn't it?..Surely he could give you some clue as to what's going on?"

"No. He said that...er..." Another sniff. "Yesterday the consulate had been telephoned by the oil company Phil works for. He, the *consulate* man, had then got in touch with the Libyan authorities and they confirmed that they did have a Phil Harley in custody for questioning." A sob. "He said he couldn't give me any more information but would be in touch. He left me his name and number and that was it!"

For a moment I remained silent, trying to digest the information. Without knowing any of the facts about the situation it was difficult to know what to say or do. If indeed, there was anything we could do. Frantically, I tried to think of a way to reassure her.

"I don't understand it," Di repeated "How can he have been arrested? He's just an engineer working for an oil company!" She paused, waiting for reassurance but none was forthcoming.

" Er..," I sighed then voiced my thoughts. "Di I'm at a loss to know what to say..."

"*But what can he have been arrested for?*" She persisted, her voice thick with emotion.

I went for a pragmatic approach trying to remain upbeat. Di needed to stay positive. "Maybe it's a mistake. You know what they're like in those countries. Arrest first then ask questions later."

"D'you think?" she sounded doubtful. "I just don't...er...can't get my head around it" she faltered. Her voice small.

"Look, I'll come over later this morning...once I'm sorted out here...we'll try to make some sense of it"

"Would you?"

"Of course. In the meantime, I know it'll be difficult but try not to worry. We'll see if we can get more information from the consulate in a couple of hours."

Her voice trembled.

"Right...I'll see you later then." She ended the call.

I sat and reflected for a few moments. The news had disturbed me. Di and Phil were old friends and I hated the thought of anything bad happening to either of them. But surely it couldn't be right. There had to have been a mistake.

Trying to force the content of Di's phone call to the back of my mind I showered and dressed then put a sweater on over a tee shirt, in case the cool early morning turned into another warm sunny day. As I opened the shutters I resolved not to become prone to negative thoughts related to *'what if scenarios?'* I needed to remain focussed on the mundane tasks of the day. So, after opening up the house to let in the morning light, I checked the time on the kitchen clock, picked up my purse and headed for the lane.

Crossing over from the courtyard toward the bend in the road out of the hamlet, I felt the sun on the back of my neck. It was just before eight and the sun was still low in the sky but it was shining brightly and was already warm. It had the makings of another beautiful day and I was determined to remain optimistic.

Rounding the corner I saw the bread van just pulling up. I approached the counter while enjoying the aroma of freshly baked bread and looked hungrily at the array of patisseries. Marie honked the horn a couple of times to let the whole hamlet know she was there then came to the counter to serve.

"*Bonjour* Marie!"

I smiled up at her, looking forward to our morning pleasantries.

Marie was an attractive woman in her early forties though she looked a good deal younger. She had short black wavy hair which always looked perfectly coiffured as well as a trim figure which often drew admiring glances. She was always cheerful, despite her frequent complaints about her lazy husband, Jean, who apparently spent all his time drinking in the bar with his friends. Marie and Jean had not been able to have children and she had confided in me once that she believed this to be the cause of his drinking. She believed his deep rooted sadness was numbed by *pastis*.

"*Bonjour* Catherine," (she pronounced it 'Catareen') "*fait beau ah?*" she smiled happily.

"*Oui, ca va?*" Her carefree demeanor was like a breath of fresh air.

"*Bien. Beaucoup du clients?*" fishing for information I suspected.

"*Oui.*" I didn't want to discuss it at that moment and was reluctant to tell her that I didn't have as many as I would like. Although I considered Marie a friend, providing good, jovial company, she also liked to gossip and tended to let everyone know everyone else's business. Any news that she had would spread like wildfire around the community.

I asked for two *baguettes* and half a dozen *croissants.* Passing them to me she asked if I would be going to the fête later. Maybe she was trying to figure out why I wasn't buying as much as I usually did. Or maybe I was just being paranoid. Maybe she was genuinely interested. Noticing my hesitation she said,

"*On pourrait avoir des boissons et des repas ensemble?*" she looked at me hopefully after proposing that we could have a meal and a few drinks together.

"*Oui, d'accord,*" I agreed.

It would be pleasant, shooting the breeze with pleasant company, good food, drinks and music on such a lovely day. The fête had proved to be very enjoyable on past occasions so there was no reason for it to be otherwise today. Yet the fact remained, I was urgently needed at Di's house.

"*J'ai un rendezvous ce matin chez mon amie, mais peut etre j'y sera plutard.*" I told her it would have to be later as I needed to go to a friend's house.

"Oh...ok..." She looked slightly dejected.

"*Peut être...Quinze heures?*" I should be back by about three at the latest I thought. I didn't think I could console Di for much longer than a couple of hours. On proposing three o'clock, Marie recovered her smile.

"*Oui, à l'aprés midi. Bonne journée.*" She turned to Monsieur Ferret, a little old man who had suddenly appeared at my left elbow. Barely reaching my shoulder in height, Monsieur Ferret had only a few wisps of grey hair and leathery weather beaten skin. Despite his very old age, he was still quite sturdy and I suspected he had spent all his working life outdoors. He lived on his own in a small house near the junction of the main road into the hamlet. I often saw him tending his vegetable patch which was closer to my house than his but never got much conversation out of him. Although I was always trying to improve my French by chatting to the locals, I found him difficult to understand. Marie had told me once that he spoke mainly '*patois*' which was some sort of local dialect. He was currently eyeing some delicious looking pastries with what looked like a custard filling. I sensed that he was itching to interrupt.

I smiled and said bonjour. He looked at me briefly, his eyes watchful though not unfriendly and muttered simply "*Madame.*"

Shrugging off this encounter, I turned and made my way back to the house. On crossing the courtyard I noticed the front door of the gîte was ajar and the boot of Frederic's car was open. Frederic, was my guest who had been staying in the gîte with his wife and two young children for nearly two weeks. A pleasant family from Paris, both husband and wife spoke impeccable English. As I walked past, Frederic came out of the house carrying two heavy looking holdalls which he hoisted into the boot. He looked preoccupied and hadn't noticed me at all.

"*Bonjour!*" I called cheerfully as I passed. He looked up, frowning.

"Oh Catherine." He came toward me so I walked over to meet him halfway.

"I am glad to 'ave seen you because we 'ave to leave early." He looked rather miserable.

"Oh I'm sorry to hear that. Has everything been ok?"

"Yes." He sighed. "We 'ave ad news of a burglary at our apartment in Paris".

"Oh no! How awful!"More bad news.

"Has anything been taken? Any damage?" I asked concerned.

"We're not sure." he shook his head perplexed. "The police contacted me last night but just said that there was a lot of mess so of course we decided to cut the 'oliday short." He pulled a face. "Luckily, it's only a couple of days. The children 'ave had such a good time ere."

As if on cue, we heard the raised voices of the children coming from inside the gîte.

"Well I hope you've enjoyed your holiday up till now. And hopefully when you get home, it won't be as bad as expected," trying to offer some consolation.

"Yes", he nodded absent mindedly, still looking distracted. "Anyway," recovering himself, "I'll leave the key on the table in the 'allway so I don't disturb you."

"Ok, thank you. I'll let you get on then. Give my regards to your family and have a safe journey home."

I left him to finish off loading the car.

Despite trying to keep my mind on other things I could feel my mood becoming subdued once again. My guests were cancelling, Phil had been arrested and now a burglary. What next?   I wished Karl was home. Sceptical though he might be, he could usually find humour in any situation and would always cheer me up no matter how dire things became.

CHAPTER FOUR

Sophie had asked if I would wake her with a knock at the door at eight thirty that morning in case she overslept so I busied myself preparing her breakfast prepared. As she was now my only guest I decided it was easier to serve breakfast in her room rather than the dining room so I could leave as soon as possible to get to Di's house. I brewed some fresh coffee and warmed a couple of *croissants*, cut up one of the crusty *baguettes* which still retained its heat from being freshly baked and put these on a tray together with a glass of fresh orange juice, a miniature pot of strawberry jam and two small individually wrapped rectangles of butter.

I knocked on the door to Sophie's room and she responded swiftly, dressed in pink spotted pyjamas. She was bleary eyed and peered at me curiously at first but then her face quickly changed to a look of sheer delight as she caught sight of the breakfast tray. I was grateful for the cheerful response.

"Morning" I said brightly, masking how I really felt.

"Oh that smells delicious!" She yawned and stepped back to let me through the doorway. I placed the tray on the bedside table pushing aside a paperback of some Swedish thriller. Sophie sank down on the bed still looking somewhat groggy.

"I had such a good night's sleep." She yawned and stretched her arms out in front of her. "It's so quiet here... and so dark!"

"Yes that definitely helps." I agreed moving back toward the door. "I have to go out this morning so won't be around till later. If you're looking for something to do there's a fête on in the village."

"Oh?" she looked down at the tray and began pouring the coffee.

"Yes, there's a market on every month. But as it's the first of the year this one's a bit special. Apart from stalls selling all sorts of food and drinks, clothes and so on, there's also music. The stall holders tend to disappear by late afternoon but the local cafés and restaurants stay open longer and have special deals to entice people in. In fact the festivities can go on till quite late."

"Mmm, sounds good," she said looking up as she bit into a *croissant*.

"I'll be there by about three so if you need company I'll look out for you or maybe see you back here later. I'll leave it up to you."

I certainly didn't want it to seem like I was telling her what do. It was her time to spend however she liked.

"Mmm..." She swallowed her food, nodding, "I might chill out for a while and then decide. But it sounds like a good idea."

Her attention turned once more to buttering a piece of bread.

"Ok, see you later then" I went to pull the door closed "And *bon appetit!*" I added with a smile before closing it completely.

Unable to reply with a mouth full of bread, she raised a hand to to wave in response.

I breathed a huge sigh as I left Sophie's room. Now I could divert my thoughts completely to Di's predicament. Reflecting on how helpless she must feel, I tried to convince myself that Phil's arrest must be a mistake and hoped that any misgivings I had were due to the influence of my low mood.

There were a few unwashed dishes in the kitchen sink but I decided other matters were more pressing so I picked up my keys and handbag, checked I had my mobile phone, locked the hall door and headed out to the car.

It's a fairly direct route from my house to Di's, the meandering country road is always quiet. Although there is a smattering of large detached houses here and there along the way, pedestrians were usually few and far between no matter what time of day. Due to my distracted thoughts I failed to notice the leafy hedgerows and spring flowers which had been so obvious the day before. The purpose of the journey left me feeling bereft of any appreciation for the natural beauty of the countryside.

On reaching Di's house I noticed the dry stone wall which bordered the property was still in need of repair – a job which she often said needed sorting out. Partially covered in ivy and adorned with pale blue shutters, the house itself sat well back from this wall and rather grandly between two fairly large outbuildings. One had been converted into an artist's studio and it was from there that I would normally have expected Di to emerge. The other building was an old broken down barn. I pulled the car in to park in front of this just as Di came scurrying from the house.

Her eyes were red and tears streamed down her face. "*It's ok!*" she cried, her look was one of great relief.

I looked at her uncomprehendingly as she pulled out a tissue from her sleeve to wipe her nose.

"He wasn't arrested, just questioned!" pausing to take a deep breath "They've actually apologised to him for the way in which he was manhandled and taken to the police station."

"Oh that's great news!" Feeling genuinely pleased as well as relieved, we embraced warmly.

Di gave a great sigh as if to stem off further tears and pulled away from me to speak.

"This last couple of hours has been a nightmare." A small sob escaped. "I couldn't help thinking about all the terrible things they do to people out there."

"Well it's over now." I rubbed her shoulder soothingly, "Let's go indoors and you can fill me in on the details."

Once inside, Di regained some of her composure as she busied herself with the day to day activity of putting the kettle on to boil.

We then sat down together at the table as she prepared to enlighten me with the details. It turned out that one of the interpreters who worked for the company and was used by a lot of staff on the compound had been found dead - hanged in her apartment. Although it looked initially like suicide, the policeman in charge suspected foul play but of course Phil hadn't been privy to the reason why. I was intrigued.

"So, what has that to do with Phil?"

"Apparently he was one of the last people to see her. So they wanted to question him to find out what he knew."

She got up to pour boiling water into the teapot, then stirred the water in it as she spoke.

"When one of his workmates saw the way he was bundled off to the police station he assumed he'd been arrested and alerted his employers. The employers then got in touch with the British Consulate."

"I see," although I didn't really.

Di sensed my confusion and continued.

"The girl who died was the interpreter," she looked at me expectantly, tea cup in hand.

I was none the wiser and shrugged my shoulders.

"You know, *the scarf!*" She paused waiting for me to catch up.

The penny eventually dropped as I thought back to our conversation the previous day.

"*Oh, right! Oh my god!*" I said, horrified.

We both fell silent as we digested the awful news.

Di glanced around the room absentmindedly

"Incidentally, I don't even know where I've put it."

I followed her thoughts and recalled picking up the scarf.

"I think I've got it in my bag. You left it on the chair in the café," I said vaguely as I pulled my bag toward me and rummaged through the contents.

Seeing it wasn't there, it dawned on me that I'd picked up a different bag in my haste to leave the house that morning.

"Oh I forgot, it's in my other bag," I said, trying to recall where I'd left it.

"Well, it's not important." Di shook her head "I can get it later. Anyway," she continued, "Phil heard on the compound that the girl's brother had been one of the insurgents involved in overthrowing Gaddaffi." She paused to let this information sink in. "Her brother was killed recently...I don't know how...but according to the rumours on the compound...it was one of the other insurgents, his sort of brothers in arms that killed him."

"Strange." It didn't make any sense to me but then I didn't know anything about the political struggles in Libya. I thought about the scarf.

"Wasn't the interpreter leaving to go back home or something? ... Wasn't that the reason she gave Phil the scarf?"

"Supposedly...she shrugged, her voice trailing off as she gave up on trying to make sense of it. "Unfortunately she never made it".

Again we fell silent, presumably both mulling over the sad ending of a life.

"I wonder if the same people killed her then?"

Di shook her head.

"Who knows? But it doesn't matter now anyway, as long as Phil's safe that's all I'm bothered about. "

She got up and went to open the refrigerator, peering inside.

I was suddenly struck by how easily we could dismiss the lives and deaths of people in another world just because we didn't know them personally. Though it was a sad reflection on humanity I came to the conclusion that it was probably for the best – otherwise we'd all carry the weight of the world on our shoulders.

Putting all thoughts of unpleasantness from her mind and focussing instead on the mundane, Di said

"Would you like a sandwich? I haven't eaten at all yet."

Sensing Di had reverted to her usual self I allowed myself to be chivvied along by her light heartedness, keen to feel much brighter.

"Actually me neither – I skipped breakfast so I'd love one."

CHAPTER FIVE

I left Di's house with my general mood much improved. I tried to persuade her to return with me to the fête but she said she was keen to finish off a painting that she wanted to show in the exhibition room. I realized after I left that I'd forgotten to ask about her mystery client - the one she'd rushed away from the café to meet the day before. Her mind had been on other things so it was understandable that she'd also forgotten to tell me about it.

I steered the car out onto the narrow lane which led to the main road. Within seconds I became conscious of a silver coloured car following closely behind -so close it must have been just inches from the bumper. The increasing noise of its engine revving led me to assume the driver was in some desperate hurry to get past. As the road was very narrow I pulled my car across to the side. It meant I was driving on the grass verge but it was the only thing I could do to let it pass. In spite of this, the car stayed behind, still very close. I peered into the rear view mirror trying to gauge who was driving but couldn't distinguish any features. The sun visor was pulled down so I could only make out a neck and shoulders but the driver was clearly male. Slowly approaching the junction to the main road, I contemplated pulling the car over to a complete stop well before it. That would force him to pass. As if reading my thoughts he suddenly pulled alongside before slowing his car to keep pace with mine. *What on earth was he doing?* From the corner of my eye I saw the driver turn his head to look directly at me. Though the car was still moving slowly I ventured a wary glance toward him, utterly bewildered by his actions. Now he was blocking the road completely. On the wrong side of the road and a danger to traffic turning at the junction. Both our cars slowed to a virtual stop as we crawled closer to the junction. Conscious of being alone in the car, I didn't want to provoke any kind of aggression yet he continued to stare brazenly at me and I caught a sneer creeping across his face. Reaching the junction, I pressed my foot down firmly on the brake to stop the car. He followed suit. I anxiously returned his look, taking in his dark, heavy-set features and malevolent looking eyes. If his intention was to intimidate it was certainly succeeding as I suddenly became conscious of my mouth drying and my heart beginning to race. Since he was making no attempt to move I considered my options. I could try to make a u-turn at the junction and return to Di's but this wasn't ideal as he could easily use his car to block the path. I could pull away at speed and head to the nearest populated area but this could be a good few miles away and I didn't like the idea of him being in a position where he could force me off the road. Glancing toward the junction I made the split decision to attempt the latter.

Putting the gear stick into reverse, my foot moved to press the accelerator but then my plan was suddenly thwarted as he pulled his car in front of mine. Gripped with panic, I hit the brake to avoid a collision. Then unexpectedly, as if he was having a sudden change of mind, he turned the car and sped off from the junction not even checking for oncoming traffic. Immediately my panic subsided though my hands were trembling as I pulled on the handbrake and sank back into the seat. Relief washed over me. I questioned my actions. What had I done to merit such treatment? Was I at fault for blocking his path? Was he simply a passing lunatic? I had a sneaking suspicion there was something unsettlingly familiar about him. Had I seen him before? Did he have a grudge against me for something I had done to him? And where had he come from anyway? Di's house was at the end of the lane and there were no other houses up there. There was no reason to be there. I took a few deep breaths, annoyed with myself for letting someone else's idiotic behaviour get to me. This was just a small incident being made into something huge because of other concerns on my mind: I must try to remain focused on the positive. Determined to have an end to it, I turned on the radio. Listening to the babble of the French radio presenter who spoke so fast I could only catch every other word wasn't going to help. I needed some lively music to take my mind off things so I pushed in a CD and turned up the volume; an old Bruce Springsteen album should do the trick. I pulled the car away from the junction. This incident would not spoil my day.

Reaching the village with only a few minutes to spare, and feeling a lot less stressed after singing my heart out to Bruce's old songs, I avoided the diversion signs and parked in a side street. Although it was still warm, the days had been cooling toward late afternoon. I didn't want to have to return to the car so I pushed a sweater into my bag then looked into the rear view mirror to check my reflection as I ran a brush through my hair, applied lipstick and a squirt of perfume. I then headed toward the main square for the first social event of the year in the *L'Absie* village calendar.

On hearing the voices of people mingling as I got closer to the hustle and bustle, my mood lifted considerably. I wondered whether the unseasonably warm weather had brought a lot more people to the fête this year than was usual. The anticipation of summer would certainly make the atmosphere more jovial. Moving closer towards the crowds I felt excitement in the air.

The main square looked just as busy as I remembered it from the previous year. The area which was normally used as a car park for visitors was taken up with stalls. A lot of the clothing stalls had only a few items left and were getting ready to close up. At one side of the square stood the railway station. The steps in front of its decorative façade were a great attraction for the youngsters. It gave them somewhere to hang out with friends among the action. They also seemed to be the main customers of a stall set up nearby to sell sandwiches and soft drinks. This was obviously much easier on the pocket. Teenagers presumably wouldn't have the money to spend in the cafés and restaurants nearby.

Directly opposite the station was the *maire's* office. It had recently been given a makeover for the occasion. The large main doors at the front had been given a new coat of dark blue glossy paint and there were huge hanging baskets filled with brilliantly coloured flowers hanging from every available outcropping.

The large grassy area beyond the car park was normally a blissfully quiet area. It was always well tended in the spring and summer months with a colourful array of plants and shrubs. A few wooden benches were dotted here and there for people to enjoy the quiet. Today, though, this area had been designated for the band. A band which was currently being set up by various people carrying equipment to and fro. Thick black electrical cabling lay across the ground like a mass of writhing snakes. It made me ponder whether any health and safety officials were involved in the setup or, indeed, if they'd even been notified.

Surrounding the stalls on the two remaining sides of the square sat a multitude of cafes and restaurants interspersed with several small shops. The shops included a *coiffeur* (hairdresser), a newsagent, an *immobilier* (estate agent) and a boutique. There were tables spilling out onto the pavements from the cafes. Most of the places were full to the brim with waiters and I marveled at how easily they weaved their way in and out of tables, balancing plates full of delectable looking food toward their hungry diners.

Making my way past the stalls I felt a little disappointed to have not been there earlier, but it was probably for the best. I would have been lured into buying far too much foodstuff than I actually needed. It always looked so delicious and far too difficult to resist.

The smell of food as I made my way through the throng to the *Hotel d'Etoile* was enough to make my mouth water. I caught a glimpse of a mop of dark hair and identified Marie standing next to an empty table, her hand holding onto one of the chairs possessively and talking excitedly to Jacques, the owner of the hotel. Jacques was a tall man, perhaps six foot four, broad in stature. With his long moustache he reminded me of a Mexican bandit. He towered over Marie's five foot frame. From afar the exchange looked quite heated but as I knew they were old friends I assumed it was just the Gallic temperament coming into play.

To reach Marie I had to squeeze past a large group of tourists congregating around a restaurant menu board. It was at that moment I had the discomforting sense of being watched. Instinctively, I turned to look to my right where a stall holder was discussing his wares with a customer. Behind him I saw a face that I instantly recognised as *the driver!* He was staring at me quite blatantly. I felt my stomach tighten. Feeling affronted by his rudeness, anger swelled up in me and I met his gaze defiantly. After only a moment's deliberation I took a deep breath and decided to march over to him and give him a piece of my mind.

Just then I heard my name called.

"*Catereen!*"

Distracted, I looked away to see Marie beckoning me over to her table. Hesitating for only a split second, I turned back toward the driver. *He had gone!* I took a moment to scan for any sight of him but it was like he had simply vanished.

Still seething with indignation, I greeted Marie with a forced smile. As always, she saw right through me. Demanding, as we kissed on both cheeks, to know what was wrong, I sat down opposite her at the table and promptly let it all out. *Everything.* I told her about the incident with the car driver. I told her about Di's husband being arrested and about how my guests were cancelling or rushing home. I had thrown caution to the wind and unburdened myself on the one person who would have this information spread like wildfire within hours.

"*Cherie*, you take the 'ole world on your shoulders," she admonished. "Your friend's 'usband is ok now?" She looked at me for confirmation and I nodded reluctantly. "Then think no more of it! And two..."

Where was *one?*

"You 'ad a meeting with a driver, who is an *imbecile*."

Her choice of words made me smile. It wasn't exactly a meeting.

Marie leaned forward and lowered her voice.

"There are a lot of imbeciles about you know." As if telling me a great secret.

I nodded in agreement feeling a chuckle rise in my throat at her turn of phrase. Marie shrugged and continued, dismissing my anxiety with a sweep of her hand.

"As for your guests, well...you 'ave 'ad no problems before. This is just a small concern."

I made no reply, pondering her remarks.

Marie also paused, reflecting on what she had said.

"The word of the mouth is very powerful. I know you have a great place there and you look after your guests. In fact, don't you 'ave a reporter staying with you?"

Seeing my look of surprise, she grinned.

"I keep the ear to the ground *cherie*", she nodded toward the seated area of the café next door and laughed softly. "Or maybe I just chatted to 'er."

I followed her gaze. Sophie was just about to take a seat at a table. She was accompanied by none other than our friendly neighbourhood *sapeur pompier*, André.

Turning back to Marie I raised my eyebrows and gave Marie a meaningful look.

"André is a good boy," she confided, lowering her voice. "And I know that 'is father would like to see 'im settled down."

"They do make a lovely couple." I glanced at them again. They were completely engrossed in each other's company.

"She seems a decent sort." I added, my thoughts based on first impressions. "I wouldn't like to see her get hurt."

Marie didn't respond to my remark. Elbows on the table, she brought her hands together in front of her face as if to conceal her expression then nodded furtively toward the entrance at the front of the café

"Speak of the devil." Marie muttered under her breath, barely loud enough for me to hear. Curious, I attempted a surreptitious glance toward the entrance.

Monsieur Lagard, the *maire*, was purposefully striding toward us through a gap in the crowd. He was a silver haired man of medium height, probably around sixty I thought, and still a handsome man. It occurred to me how much his son resembled him. Monsieur

Lagard had recently taken to carrying a walking cane with an elaborately decorated silver lion's head on the handle. There didn't seem to be any obvious reason for needing it so I suspected he liked the distinguished look it gave him more than anything else.

"*Bonjour!* Marie! *Madame* Patterson!" He was beaming and bent to kiss us both in turn. Addressing me he said.

"It is another great success, no?" He looked around with his arms wide as if to show off the whole square.

"It's wonderful." I enthused, smiling as I realized my mood had again been lifted, "Made even better by being such a glorious day."

It was now late afternoon and the air was still warm. A few fluffy white clouds drifted slowly here and there across the beautiful blue sky.

"I agree *Madame*. And of course pretty reporters are turning 'eads."

He gestured toward Sophie and his son, André, who still hadn't noticed us or anyone else for that matter.

"Maybe your reporter will write a good story about the village as well 'uh?"

So he already knew what she did.

I laughed softly. "Yes, I'm sure she will."

Jacques, the owner, passed us on his way to a customer and Monsieur Lagard's eyes lit up.

"Jacques!" he called and then turned quickly to us "Excuse me please. I must go and attend to business. I will see you tomorrow evening *Madame* Patterson."

"Oh?" I gave him a confused look.

"Yes, I am having dinner with Monsieur and *Madame* McCoy," he explained. "I 'ave 'eard about the tunnel. I am going to give them the benefit of my extended knowledge on the subject. I will see you then. *Àdemain*."

Eager to follow after Jacques he simply nodded and scurried off toward the interior of the hotel. Marie followed him with her eyes, curious to see what he was up to.

"I wonder what is going on there?" she said quietly as if to herself. She never misses a trick I thought. Then she leaned toward me as if to share another great secret.

"You know Jacques is one of my 'usband's drinking buddies? Now he is luring 'im into gambling would you believe?" Her eyes narrowed. "Some clandestine gambling is going on 'ere and I 'ave been warning Jacques, 'e must not get Jean deeply involved."

So that was why it looked like she was arguing with him.

Marie continued. "I don't want Jean going down that route and 'e is so easily led." She let out a great sigh. "Anyway, let's forget about our troubles and order some wine."

"Sounds good to me," I smiled cheerfully and picked up the menu. "By the way, where is Jean today?"

"Oh working...always working" she shook her head and in doing so avoided my eyes.

I sensed that she didn't want to talk about it so resolved not to mention it again.

We had nearly finished our first glass of white wine before the food arrived. I had ordered a creamy chicken dish with a mélange of vegetables to go with it from a set menu. Marie ordered fish which was from the *menu du jour*, written up on the chalk board. It came with a generous helping of crusty bread. I had not realized how hungry I was until I began to tuck in. As we ate, Marie gave me the low down on the people she had seen in the hour before I'd arrived. She also showed off a pair of strappy leather sandals which she had purchased from a shoe stall. She'd changed into them as soon as she sat down at the table, putting her shoes into a carrier bag which she'd pushed into a large handbag.

"I must confess this warm weather 'as caught me off the 'op", I grinned, realising she meant 'on the hop'.

"I haven't 'ad time to get out all of my summer clothes and shoes."

While contemplating the cheese course, the music started. Marie went to 'powder the nose' as she put it, so I manoeuvered my seat around to get a better view of the square. The stalls were now long gone and people were sitting outside the cafés on plastic chairs, kerbs and any other kind of makeshift seating they could find to enjoy the music alongside the lovely weather. Though I tried to keep it from my mind, I found myself scanning the crowd once again for 'the driver'. Had he followed me? Or was it just a coincidence that he'd been there? I gave up looking after a while as I couldn't see any sign of him. It was a relief. I did catch sight of Lesley and Tim however; they were sitting with Sue on the railway station steps enjoying the music. Out of curiosity, I glanced over to where Sophie and André were spotted previously. They were gone. Just then Marie returned. She must have caught me looking.

"They left about twenty minutes ago."

"Oh?" I hadn't seen them in the crowd.

She raised her eyebrows and grinned. " 'and in 'and I noticed."

"Right." I nodded then shrugged with a smile. I wasn't about to make any assumptions, it really wasn't any of my business.

By six o'clock the band was in full swing. Our second bottle of wine had arrived and I felt relaxed physically and mentally. Knowing I only had Sophie's room to tidy, and as she probably wouldn't notice anyway, meant I could forget about the chambres d'hôtes for now and just enjoy myself. Marie, despite her propensity to gossip, was good company and made me laugh. She was also a good listener and considerate in her advice.

As the evening wore on, the sun was beginning to set and the air cool. I was glad of the sweater I had packed into my bag. The music from the band finished around eight thirty and despite my reluctance to end such a pleasant day, I decided it was time for home. Marie protested, reluctant to let me go but also conceding that she too needed to be up early so it was wise to call it a day. We said our good byes and went our separate ways. I decided to walk the short distance home rather than drive. I had had a few too many glasses of wine and knew, rather than suspected, I was over the limit.

I walked away from the main square toward a narrow path alongside the main road. It was normally about a ten minute walk, but I seemed to be having some difficulty keeping up a brisk pace. As I ambled, I envisioned the lack of street lighting on this particular road and became concerned at how it could quickly be plunged into darkness making my journey much more difficult and hazardous.

As a result, I picked up the pace and managed to reach the hamlet just as the sun disappeared over the horizon, congratulating myself on having the willpower to leave the fête sooner rather than later,. Despite the light fading fast there was still a tiny vestige of illumination from the setting sun, enough for me to make out a silver Saab parked next to Sophie's Renault in the courtyard. I assumed that Sophie had walked to the village square and wondered who the other car belonged to.

Approaching the entrance at the side of the house I saw the figure of a man ahead, standing with his back toward me as if looking out onto the garden. The diminishing light meant I could only make him out in silhouette and could not distinguish any features. There was however, something familiar about him. My heart suddenly began to race. I was alert to the fact that I was probably the only one at home in the hamlet. I hadn't noticed Lesley, Tim or Sue leave the fête but then I hadn't been looking. Maybe they were at home. Maybe they weren't!

Was it *the driver?* Was it a silver Saab that had passed me on the road? I tried desperately to recall the type of car but could only remember the colour. Silver. He was about the same height and build. *It must be him. How did he know where I lived? Had he come to make trouble? Was I in danger?* Taking a deep breath and determined not to give in to my fear I made him aware of my presence.

"Hello!" I shouted rather forcefully than expected. "Can I help you?"

He turned and strode purposefully toward me. My sudden relief was palpable as I instantly realised, despite his broad, heavy stature, it was not him. He held out his hand.

"Good evening." He searched my face. "I am sorry if I startled you *Madame*." he spoke English, but not with a french accent.

I offered my hand in greeting.

"Oh not at all!" I giggled as he took my hand and kissed it. Giggling? Was I hysterical? Yes, I thought, probably with relief. And of course too much wine.

"I just wasn't expecting anyone." I felt myself smile girlishly up at him – not something I was used to, being five feet nine inches tall - I guessed he must be a good six inches taller.

"Of course not," he said kindly. "Perhaps I should have telephoned first." He paused, looking at me steadily then continued. "I was driving to a hotel in

Niort but it was getting late and I saw your sign, so I thought...why not?" He shrugged his shoulders and waited for my response.

"Yes, I understand."

My heart was gradually beginning to quiet. I drew myself up and turned to lead him toward the entrance. "You are lucky I've had a cancellation so there's no problem, Monsieur ...?"

"Saleem," he replied.

"Is it just for one night?" I enquired.

"I think I might stay around for about three or four to sightsee in the area actually. Would that be possible?"

"Certainly."

I could have kissed him I was so pleased to have another guest. Managing to keep myself in check, I smiled gleefully as I went through the hallway to unlock the door to the house. I struggled with the key in the lock for what seemed an embarrassingly long period of time. I needed to get his room key from inside the house but the door was proving very difficult to open.

"I don't know what's wrong with this lock." I said, feeling myself redden. Again, too much wine, I thought.

"Let me help please."

Mr Saleem came over to take the key from my hand. I stood back to give him room. Swiftly and easily he opened the door.

"Oh thank you." I gratefully took back the key and he smiled down at me. He looks like Omar Sharif, I thought. Then it occurred to me that I had definitely had too much wine.

After picking up his room key, I led him round to the back of the house. I explained on the way that the entrance to the chambres d'hôtes was via the courtyard. On opening the door to his room I stood back to let him pass. He entered and surveyed the room. He wasn't carrying luggage. I assumed he'd left it in the car.

"Thank you *Madame*, it is a very pleasant room. I am sure I will be very comfortable here."

I told him breakfast was usually between eight and ten. He could let me know if he needed to eat earlier. He thanked me again. I tried to place his accent. Curiosity got the better of me as I made to leave.

"You're not French Mr Saleem. Where is it you're from?"

"Egypt." He answered simply.

Sensing he did not want to elaborate I bade him goodnight and left.

I returned to the house feeling pleased. Sophie could now view the place with other guests around. The report in the magazine would be much more positive if she could mention other guests as well as their comments.

I returned to the house and went upstairs to bed. It had been a long day. I couldn't be bothered to check for phone messages or email. Conscious of the amount of wine I had imbibed, I had two large glasses of water before quickly changing for bed. Then I collapsed, exhausted and fell into a deep sleep.

CHAPTER SIX

Friday

I woke up with a blinding headache. Sunlight streaming into the bedroom didn't help. Holding my head in my hands till I could bare to sit up, I chided myself for drinking more wine than I knew I could handle. Recalling the sudden arrival of a new guest while in that state made me cringe. What on earth must he think of me? I made a vain attempt to recall what I'd said to him, but came up mostly blank. Hopefully, I hadn't disgraced myself.

After showering for longer than usual to liven up, I eventually pulled myself around enough to get dressed, which I did slowly and methodically, no sudden movements.

A measured glance around the room just as I was leaving left me in a state of confusion. The place was not just untidy but downright messy. There were clothes hanging loosely out of several drawers on the dresser, the lid of the jewellery box on top (housing only costume jewellery I might add) was slightly ajar due to a bead necklace wedged crudely into it. The classic Louis XV style armchair which sat idly by the dresser in the corner, more for decoration than a much needed seat, was askew; the lilac beaded cushion which usually adorned it lay on the floor close by. Even the long mirror on the wall seemed crooked. Searching my memory for how the bedroom got to this state, left me feeling baffled, so I gave up. With a sigh I shook my head slowly, vowing as most people do in this state, never to drink again.

Heading downstairs I decided being teetotal would be good for me anyway, you can't run a business properly if you're drunk or hung over. I should be thinking of my reputation. Drinking to be social was okay but to excess was not good at all. I should have had the will power to refuse drinks when I'd reached my limit. I shouldn't have allowed Marie to ply me with wine. She might be immune to the effects of alcohol but I wasn't, but I shouldn't be blaming her, it's not as if she'd held a gun to my head, it was probably just my frame of mind, I'd been desperate to calm my nerves after being terrorised by some maniac. Terrorised?

That's a bit strong. I'd just overreacted to someone else's road rage.

The argument in my head came to a stop as I struggled to turn the key in the lock of the hallway door. Soon realising I'd left the door unlocked anyway, a sudden flash of memory about a problem with the lock the previous night made me redden. I'd had to rely on my new guest to open it. Had I damaged it by drunkenly trying to turn the key too forcefully? Maybe. It also became apparent that I'd left the outer door unlocked as well. Mindful of the fact that burglary in the area was virtually unheard of, I thanked my lucky stars that no harm was done.

On the way to meet the bread van I knew Karl would have no problem fixing the lock when he got back. Should I confess to breaking the lock while I was drunk? I knew Karl wouldn't be bothered but would I ever live it down? I could imagine the ribbing I'd get for years to come.

Putting the problem from my mind, I enjoyed the cool and refreshing morning breeze against my flushed face. No doubt we'd be basking in warm sunshine by midmorning if the weather from the past week was anything to go by.

On approaching the bread van I was surprised to find a young girl in place of Marie. I surmised that

Marie was probably also feeling a bit worse for wear and had therefore got someone to stand in for her. Without any of the usual banter, for which I was unusually thankful, I bought fresh bread and *croissants,* said *bonjour* to Monsieur Ferret and returned to the kitchen to prepare breakfast.

Mr Saleem appeared around eight thirty, looking freshly showered in a crisp white shirt and pale canvas trousers. I even got a waft of aftershave which seemed vaguely familiar. Karl probably had something similar.

Thankfully I was feeling more myself by this time and I realised that in the cold light of day he was perhaps not the Omar Sharif look alike I'd believed him to be. More, in fact, like a heavily set distant cousin of Omar Sharif with thinning hair.

Deciding to act business like in my manner toward him, rather than appear sheepish about any previous unseemly behaviour, I greeted Mr Saleem quite briskly with a 'good morning'. Checking whether his preference was for tea or coffee, I then made rather a hasty departure to prepare breakfast.

I returned shortly with coffee, juice, bread and croissants. If he noticed the change in my manner, now that I was sober, he was certainly gentleman enough not to show it. He offered what he said was 'another' apology for turning up without warning the previous evening and I assured him that it was not a problem and he should think no more of it. He cheerfully agreed, hopefully sensing that I would prefer not to discuss it.

Changing the subject, he enquired politely about the local area. Glad of the distraction, I chatted readily about the various places of interest he could visit. I also provided him with leaflets giving information about routes and opening times of events.

He smiled, accepting the information gratefully and I noted while we talked, even without the aid of alcohol, he still seemed charming and I warmed to his friendly manner. Keen as he was to engage me in conversation, I asked whether he'd come far the day before. He explained that he'd flown in from Cairo to Paris and was making his way to a relative's wedding in Limoges. I thought it odd that he didn't get a flight closer to where he needed to be and said so. He stated simply that as he had a few days to spare before arriving at his destination, he'd hired a car with the intention of doing a bit of sightseeing and hoping to come across accommodation on the way. Our chambres d'hôtes was the first place he'd stopped and luckily, he said, there was a room was available.

As we chatted I was suddenly struck by the coincidence of him being Egyptian and Sophie also being part Egyptian. Had my brain not been foggy from the effects of alcohol, I presumed I would have made the connection sooner. I made a mental note to mention it to Sophie later.

Finally, leaving Mr Saleem to finish his breakfast I went back to the house. Sophie had still not surfaced by ten so I decided to catch up on some paperwork. I also checked the phone messages. There was one from Karl. He said he was mainly ringing to let me know that our web site seemed to have crashed. He was wondering if I'd managed to take any bookings in spite of it. This at least explained why, when checking the emails, there hadn't been any requests for reservations. It didn't, however, account for those two cancellations. Karl also hoped I'd enjoyed the fete and said that Aidan was now with him. He remarked jokingly that Aidan had had to be restrained from raiding the mini bar when he'd arrived at the hotel because he was so hungry. He then ranted for a minute or two about students and how their money is spent on alcohol and they don't eat. He ended the call by saying that he was just about to take Aidan out to dinner and would phone on Saturday to see how things were. I smiled at the thought of them together and enjoying each other's company.

"Morning!"

I turned to see Sophie standing at the door. It was now eleven thirty which was usually too late for the breakfast which was included in the room rate. Of course Sophie was more than a paying guest.

"Good morning. Would you like breakfast?....Or would you prefer lunch?" I said amicably, smiling at her.

She looked shamefaced. "I have overslept a little haven't I?'

"It doesn't matter," I said brightly guiding her toward a seat at the kitchen table. I was secretly dying to know how her evening went but didn't feel that I knew her well enough to pry.

"How about an omelette?" I asked as she made herself comfortable. "It combines breakfast and a light lunch."

"Lovely, thanks." She went to stifle a yawn. "It was a late night." She started to explain "I met André at the fête...you know...the fireman?"

I nodded trying to look only vaguely interested.

"We had dinner." Her tone was wistful.

I turned to break the eggs into a dish and hid a smile at her obvious happiness.

"We're having dinner again tonight" she continued.

"Really?" I feigned surprise. It had been obvious they only had eyes for each other when they'd been seen at the restaurant.

"You must have really hit it off." I said as I presented her with some freshly cut bread. I didn't wait for her reply but turned my attention back to the omelette now in the pan.

"Yes…" She sighed and I turned to look at her. She was staring dreamily into space. Smitten!

After finishing her breakfast Sophie said she planned to spend the afternoon writing up some of her notes after lounging around the pool for a little while. As she was about to leave, I remembered Mr Saleem. I told her that coincidentally there was now another guest who was also Egyptian. She looked surprised and agreed that yes, it was a coincidence. She said that if she bumped into him she might try some of her rudimentary knowledge of the language on him.

CHAPTER SEVEN

It was early afternoon and I was busy munching on a sandwich when Lesley appeared at the door. She'd come to invite me to dinner and informed me that Monsieur Lagard was also expected. He would be divulging everything he knew about the tunnel in the cellar as he was, he'd told her, something of an expert. I confessed that he had mentioned dinner the day before when I'd seen him at the fête. I was also intrigued by the fact that there was a story about the tunnel and so eagerly accepted her invitation.

"The *geometre* will be here later this afternoon to have a look at the cellar so we should find out then if the house is going to collapse or not." She grimaced.

"Well, best to get things checked out, just for peace of mind. But I'm sure everything will be fine." I seemed to be finding myself saying that more and more these days.

Lesley advised me that we'd eat around seven thirty and then left me to finish off my sandwich.

Later that same afternoon I took the short walk to the village to pick up my car. On the way I called into the supermarket to buy a decent bottle of wine to take to Lesley's that evening.

Travelling back to the hamlet, I drove down the same road as I'd walked the evening before. A couple of miles before the right turn into the lane leading into the hamlet I noticed a car following in the rear view mirror. The car was silver in colour. It brought to mind the maniac driver from the day before. But this silver car was keeping well behind. Probably the recommended two or three cars distance or whatever was the equivalent in the French Highway Code.

I indicated at the turn and though there was no particular reason, began to feel a little anxious as I slowed the car to turn. Checking the mirror again to confirm the other car's whereabouts, I watched as it went straight past the turning, carrying on down the same road. Letting out a deep sigh I shook my head, rebuking myself for being paranoid. There were lots of silver cars on the road so it was silly to let my imagination get the better of me each time I saw one.

Minutes later I pulled the car into the courtyard, deducing that Mr Saleem must be engaged in some sightseeing activity since his car was nowhere to be seen. On the way into the house I caught a glimpse of

Sophie relaxing on a sun lounger by the pool. Seeing as they were both out and about I decided it was an ideal time to make up both their rooms.

Once in the chambre d'hotes I picked up clean towels from the airing cupboard on the landing and armed myself with extra toiletries for the bathrooms. I then went into each room to make up the bed, empty the bin and ensure surfaces were clean and tidy. I then did a quick appraisal to satisfy myself that I'd left the rooms looking presentable before closing each door.

Leaving the chambres d'hôtes I saw Mr Saleem's car parked in the courtyard and thought it fortunate that I had managed to get into his room in the short time he had been out.

Carrying a bag of rubbish and a pile of used towels back to the house, I thought of taking some time to clean the gîte. Despite not having anyone booked to stay there until June, I had decided I might as well have it cleaned and ready. It would then only need a quick dust over before someone arrived. I could be inundated with requests once the website was working again, I thought ruefully, unsure if I should be allowing myself to be so optimistic.

On the way back to the house I observed Sophie and Mr Saleem talking by the pool. She was lying, propped up on an elbow on the lounger and was looking up at him as she shielded her eyes from the sun. He was sitting down on another lounger opposite. They were too far away for me to hear their conversation but I wondered if perhaps she was asking him among other things about his stay as part of her research for the magazine article.

I went into the house to put the towels into the small laundry room which was adjacent to the kitchen. I kept a large plastic bucket there which contained all of the cleaning materials I usually needed for the gîte. Carrying the mop in one hand and the bucket in the other I stepped outside and nearly collided with Sophie.

"Oops!" I stepped back a little, surprised at the briskness of her pace.

Sophie seemed completely absorbed in her own thoughts, hardly noticing that she had nearly sent me flying.

"Sorry. My fault." She looked blank, her voice flat.

"No harm done." I said cheerfully expecting her to stay for a moment and make small talk.

Uncharacteristically, she simply nodded and muttered that she had a few phone calls to make then went on her way. I was taken aback at her manner, believing that we had been quickly becoming friends. For a few moments I stared after her, curious. Then I looked instinctively towards Mr Saleem who, from the way he was now standing had been watching the interaction between me and Sophie just seconds earlier.

The hard look on Mr Saleem's face surprised me and I wondered at the conversation between him and Sophie which just a few minutes ago I'd judged to be affable enough. Could there have been a disagreement? Such strong emotions between two people who didn't know each other seemed odd. After a moment or two Mr Saleem became aware of me studying him and his face changed swiftly, breaking into a smile. He waved hello and I responded with a nod and held up my hands slightly to show him they were full, as if to explain for not returning his wave. He nodded in understanding and then sat down on a lounger with his back to me. I continued to watch him for a little while longer, confused about what had just occurred. He took a few moments to get himself comfortable, putting his feet up and lying back then turned his face in the direction of the sun.

Carrying on with my chores I headed for the gîte, all the time speculating about what might have happened. Had I been witness to something more sinister than just a clash of words? Sophie was an attractive girl. She'd been wearing a strapless top and shorts. Maybe Mr Saleem, being used to women covering up, had mistaken Sophie's attire as evidence she was available and willing. An improper advance could certainly account for her distress. I shrugged. This was all supposition. Maybe she would tell me herself later.

I didn't see Sophie or Mr Saleem for the rest of the afternoon. My time was taken up cleaning the gîte.

Just after six I showered and changed for dinner at Lesley's. Putting on a long flowing white skirt and pink blouse, it looked feminine and smart but still casual enough to be comfortable. I looked in the mirror to put on mascara and lipstick and noticed that I'd caught the sun. My face and arms were lightly tanned and my shoulder length, mousy brown hair had lightened considerably. I looked vibrant and healthy and it made me feel quite pleased with myself.

As I was ready well before time I sat for a while on the terrace enjoying the warm evening air and looking out across the garden to the hills beyond. The air was so still and quiet. I tried to decide whether this time of day or early morning was my favourite. I did miss someone to share it with though and looked forward to Karl returning from London.

After appreciating the view for a while my mind drifted back to my lack of guests and wondered if things would pick up soon. Perhaps we'd just been lucky for the first few years. Maybe this year was how it was normally supposed to be. Or maybe, as Karl would say, I shouldn't be trying to predict how the season would work out.

My mind drifted to other events from the last few days. The driver who had followed me from Di's then turned up at the fête. Could that have been simply coincidence? Then what about Mr Saleem? When he turned up out of the blue on Thursday evening I'd actually thought he was the same driver! Yes, my memory had that stored away despite the alcohol. What an idiot I was, frightening myself like that! And then again today, imagining I could be being followed again just because the car behind was silver. My God, Catherine, you really need to get a grip.

Deciding I'd sat too long with my own thoughts for my own good, I checked the time on the clock in the lounge. It was just before seven. I picked up the bottle of wine, locked the french doors and outer door of the house and headed across to Lesley's for dinner.

I was about to cross the road when I saw Sophie heading to her car looking very elegant in a red knee length wrapped dress that showed off her slim figure. With her olive skin and very little makeup, apart from pale pink lipstick, she looked stunning. Realising she hadn't seen me I stopped and called over to her.

"Wow, you look like you're dressed to kill!"

She looked towards me in surprise. A huge grin spread across her face, obviously flattered.

"Thanks, that's the intended outcome," she laughed.

Back to her usual self then. I watched for a moment as she carried on walking toward her car, keys in hand. Suddenly she stopped as if remembering something. Turning, she came toward me frowning. I gave her a questioning look but said nothing. Slowing as she came toward me, she took a moment to speak as if gathering her thoughts. Then, leaning in close, her hand touched my arm as her voice sank to a whisper.

"I need to speak to you later." She paused to look around as if checking there was no one within earshot.

"Sounds very cloak and dagger" I joked casually.

Her face was solemn, "it's a serious matter actually." She looked down at her watch. "I don't have the time now but I'll see you tomorrow."

"Ok," I was intrigued. What was the great secret? Was it something to do with Mr Saleem? To do with what had occurred earlier? She obviously didn't want to talk about it now so I didn't ask.

Trying to lighten the mood I said cheerily "Well, till then, have a great time!"

She recovered her smile "Yes, I'm sure I will."

I watched as she turned and walked towards her car. Seconds later, Mr Saleem appeared from around the corner. He was dressed in a light grey suit with white open neck shirt. He looked very smart and had a determined look on his face as he walked briskly toward his own car. I wondered if he was on his way to a hot date as well. While observing them both, it struck me as rather odd that neither Sophie nor Mr Saleem acknowledged the others presence, yet by their proximity, they had to be both acutely aware of each other.

In fact it looked as if they were making a conscious effort to ignore one another. I continued to wonder at this lack of civility as I watched Sophie pull her car out of the hamlet. Her face now obviously quite set made me feel even more curious about what had happened.

Caught up in my own thoughts I watched her car disappear then glanced momentarily toward Mr Saleem. I was a little unnerved to find he was regarding me with much interest.

His look, on seeing that I had a bottle of wine in my hand, changed to one of amusement. I suddenly felt very self-conscious. What on earth must he think? Off to another drinking session?

He lifted his hand briefly in greeting as he went to open the car door. I nodded and smiled but said nothing and turned to head across the road to Lesley's house.

CHAPTER EIGHT

"Catherine!" Tim opened the door his arms wide and greeted me like a long lost friend. It was heart warming.

"Come in, come in". He gave me a bear hug and we kissed on both cheeks. I noted he'd put on weight. He wasn't a tall man. In fact he was probably a few inches shorter than me so his weight gain was fairly obvious. He was fair haired and had a ruddy complexion and the extra weight made him look jolly.

I offered him the bottle of wine. He sucked air in through his lips as he studied the label.

"A good year." He seemed impressed.

"I thought it might be a small consolation for some of the wine you've lost"

"Thank you." He seemed touched. "It was very thoughtful."

Ushering me in through the kitchen, I detected the wonderful aroma of home cooked food which made my mouth water. I was starving and it made me think about Karl. He would chastise me if he knew I wasn't eating properly. When I was left on my own, I would often skip meals and just snack when I felt hungry. It was something Karl often took issue with.

Tim led me into the dining room where I found Monsieur Lagard and Lesley. With a glass of red wine already in hand, the *maire* was enthusing about the previous day's events. I also noticed he was still holding onto his lion headed cane. They both turned to greet me as I entered.

"*Madame!*" "Catherine!" They chorused. More kisses on cheeks.

"Wine?" Lesley asked and went toward a large french dresser which stood against one wall. She poured out a glass of rosé which she knew I preferred.

"Thanks." So my resolve had crumpled easily. Drink exceedingly slowly tonight, I told myself.

Glancing around the room I said, "It's lovely in here."

Lesley smiled to acknowledge my compliment.

"We finished this room just before we left last autumn...that's probably why you haven't seen it yet."

Two opposing walls were made of sandstone blocks and the exposed stone shown as a feature. The other two walls were plastered with cream coloured *crepi*, an unevenly finished plaster which was a characteristic of homes in the area. The warmth of the yellow stone and creamy walls gave the room a pleasant ambience.

The garden behind the house could be seen through the large rectangular window on the far wall. The steep slope of the hill at the back of the garden was obvious. I assumed this was where the water ran down toward the house when it rained. We had purportedly had more rain this past winter for more than a century, so it was no wonder the cellar had flooded.

As it was quickly becoming dusk, Tim began lighting candles around the room. There were four small niches in the sandstone walls which housed large round white candles. After lighting those, he stood, somewhat precariously, I thought, on a chair to reach up toward a chandelier. The circular chandelier which hung from the ceiling toward the centre of a large farmhouse style table had a dozen or so candles arranged evenly around its circumference. It was a beautiful, decorative focal point above the table, and now that the air was cooling, the candle light gave off heat as well as a pleasingly warm glow.

Though the colours of the walls, ceilings and floor were neutral, Lesley had used accessories in various shades of green around the room in an attempt to liven up the décor and add interest. This included large green raffia place mats placed on the table upon which sat heavy stainless steel cutlery. The drinking glasses were tinged with a green hue and sparkled as the light from the candles reflected in the crystal. An array of condiments sat in a long shallow green raffia tray placed at the centre of the table. It was all very tasteful.

Tim left the room for a few minutes while Lesley poured out drinks but returned promptly with a tray of attractive looking *canapés*. These consisted of small pieces of salmon placed in sour cream on a small round cracker. They were garnished with the tiniest sprinkling of rosemary and looked delicious.

Lesley gestured for me and Monsieur Lagard to take our seats at the table. I was glad to see Tim place a large carafe of water nearby and I helped myself freely to a glass. Meanwhile Monsieur Lagard continued the conversation he had already started with Lesley about the great success of the fête. I agreed that it had been a marvellous day and commented that it was putting *L'Absie* on the map, an observation with which he eagerly concurred.

After we consumed all but a couple of the *canapés* and exhausted the conversation about the fête, Lesley told us about the *geometre* and the advice she and Tim been given about the tunnel.

Apparently, the house was stable but it would be better to get the tunnel blocked because it could flood again. The *geometre* had said that if it were to happen too often it may become a danger and affect the foundations. Although the amount of rain we'd had last winter had been unusual, his opinion was that it may become more usual due to global warming. On his advice, Tim had contacted a company which the *geometre* had recommended. The workers from the company would be there early Monday morning to pour in the concrete. Lesley said she would be leaving the key with the farmer next door, Monsieur Sabiron. She explained that they wouldn't be back till about ten on Monday morning because they would be picking up their daughter, son-in-law and two grandchildren from the airport. As it was such an early morning flight they were leaving on Sunday to spend the day in La Rochelle and stay overnight.

"I was telling your guest about it all...er...Mr Saleem is it?"

I nodded.

"A very charming man. He seemed very interested." said Lesley.

"Is he middle eastern?" interrupted Tim.

"Egyptian apparently." The Egyptian connection between Mr Saleem and Sophie came to mind. I wondered again what had taken place.

"Does he live in France then?" enquired Lesley.

I focussed on Lesley's question putting the Sophie and Mr Saleem incident from my mind.

"No, just flew in. Said he's going to some family celebration and just passing through this way. Wanted to do a bit of sight-seeing on the drive down to his relative's house."

"Oh." Lesley nodded as she digested the information. Now fully cognisant, she changed the subject. Turning to Monsieur Lagard she said."Tim and I have been to some of the troglodyte caves in *Meschers*."

Monsieur Lagard nodded, politely interested.

"I wondered if the caves and tunnels there were used for the same reason you mentioned about the tunnel under the house?" She paused. "You know, the er...Vendéen wars?"

"Not precisely. In fact, the caves at *Meschers* were in'abited throughout the centuries. They were a refuge for the Protestants in the religious wars of the sixteenth and seventeenth centuries." Monsieur Lagard explained with an air of authority, sounding very much like the expert he purported to be. "If you want to see other troglodyte caves, there are some at *La Doué Fontaine*."

Tim excused himself and went to the kitchen to check on the food.

"*La Doué Fontaine?* Isn't that fairly close to here?" Lesley looked at me for confirmation. I, in turn, looked at Monsieur Lagard who I thought was probably the best one to ask.

"I think so." I said, not quite sure of myself.

"Yes, of course." Monsieur Lagard confirmed. "You can be there in less than one hour." He took a sip of wine.

"Well then. How about it Catherine?" she looked at me expectantly.

I shrugged, feeling slightly ambushed, but not averse to the idea of a day sightseeing. I said "Why not? When do you want to go?"

"What about tomorrow? Tim is going to mow the lawn and tidy the garden up a bit and I want some time to myself before the family arrive."

It would certainly take my mind off my lack of guests.

"Okay." I said thoughtfully, I still had to be around to serve breakfast. " Elevenish?"

"Great!"

At that moment Tim arrived with the food. He was dragging several dishes on what appeared to be some sort of hostess trolley. Seeing Lesley's cheerful expression he said "What have I missed?"

Lesley got up to help with the dishes.

"Catherine and I are off to look at some caves tomorrow. We're leaving you alone to your garden."

He looked at me. A look of genuine relief on his face.

"Rather you than me," he muttered quietly from the corner of his mouth as he passed me by to place the dishes onto the table. And then louder still, "To be quite frank, I think once you've seen one lot of caves you've seen 'em all. So, I'm quite happy not to be tagging along. And besides I love pottering around in the garden on my own."

I looked at Monsieur Lagard to gauge his response. I knew him to be a keen ambassador for the area. His face was expressionless. If he was irritated by what Tim had said, he didn't show it.

Lesley took the lids off the dishes which had just been set upon the table. She announced that one of them was a dish of sliced chicken served in a peppery cream sauce. There was no need for any further explanation: the smell of garlic from a large bowl of small potatoes spoke for itself. Next to that were dishes of asparagus, peas and carrots. The food looked absolutely delicious. I filled up my plate and began to eat with relish. Both myself and Monsieur Lagard paid compliments to the chef.

The conversation during the meal stayed light and I found the company entertaining. It was turning into a very pleasurable evening.

After we had finished our main course, Lesley turned to Monsieur Lagard who was looking very satisfied and a little flushed after eating such a hearty meal.

"I am dying to know what the tunnel was built for..." she glanced at me and then back to Monsieur Lagard. "I have imagined all sorts of things, but to my shame... I must confess... I know little of the history of the area.

I remained silent as I felt slightly guilty that my own knowledge was severely lacking.

"To understand about the tunnels," Monsieur Lagard began "first you must 'ave some knowledge of the region."

By attempting to draw out as much of the background detail as possible, it soon became obvious that Monsieur Lagard considered himself to be something of a raconteur. He appeared to be in his element as we gave him our undivided attention. Explaining that he wanted us to have a feeling for the mood of the time.

"You know of course about the revolution." He waited till the three of us confirmed this before continuing.

"At the time of the revolution this," he spread his arms wide, "was a poor rural area. It was in'abited by peasants and poor priests."

He looked at the three of us to ensure we were following.

"There were petit bourgeoisies and aristocrats but they were impoverished as well. This poverty meant that there was not as much social inequality 'ere as elsewhere in France."

Sitting back in his chair Monsieur Lagard paused as if for dramatic effect. He was enjoying his position at centre stage.

"You must understand that the *Vendée* was staunchly royalist..."

"Ah yes," interrupted Tim enthusiastically. This had obviously sparked his interest. "Isn't this where Richard the Lion Heart had a castle?"

Monsieur Lagard looked pleased with Tim's knowledge. "His *main* castle...*oui*... at *Talmont St.Hilaire.*"

He then lowered his voice as if telling a great secret.

"His mother was Eleanor of Aquitaine. She was born at *Nieul-sur-l'Autise.* You know it?..." Lesley and I exchanged glances then nodded uncertainly. Monsieur Lagard detected our hesitation.

"Just outside of *Fontenay le Comte*," he explained. "In the South of the *Vendée*." He paused as if to give us time to digest this information then continued.

"Back to the revolution...In Paris, the Republicans took control." He grasped at the air to make 'taking of control' more dramatic. He paused again for a moment. I suspected that if we kept interrupting we'd never find out about the tunnels. Perhaps the others thought so too because the three of us then sat silently, giving him our full attention. He continued.

"They, the new Republican state, wanted control of the church. So... they confiscated its property...banned traditional priests and suppressed all religious orders. The priests who refused to be under state control were outlawed and replaced by state *priests...* The state also increased taxes. Then they introduced conscription...This of course was the final straw!" He thumped the table as he made this last statement, his voice becoming impassioned.

Tim sensed a pause and jumped in.

"So are you saying this area didn't support the revolution?"

Monsieur Lagard shook his head. He didn't answer directly.

"The people of the *Vendée* did not see the great inequalities of wealth as in the rest of France. They were also a very religious people."

"I see" nodded Tim soberly.

"In 1793 Catholic churches were closed across France by the Republicans. The ordinary devout Catholic could not fulfil their religious obligations. So..." he looked at us each in turn checking to see if we understood the implication of his words, "the *Vendée Militaire*, as the rebels became known, defied conscription."

He paused to have a sip of wine.

"That sounds fascinating!" Tim interrupted again. "I wish I'd looked into the history before."

Monsieur Lagard nodded as he paused, his face deadly serious. He continued.

"Paris ordered Republican troops and National Guards to enforce conscription...To go against the rebels... Although the rebels tried valiantly to defy the government forces they unfortunately had a great weakness. They lacked a unified army..." He shook his head sadly. "*Oui*, they had some success at fighting in *Thouars*, *Saumur*, *Châtillon* and *Vihiers* against the Republican forces, but they had a very bad defeat at the battle of *Cholet*...Then there was a further terrible defeat at the port of *Granville*. Twenty five thousand rebels arrived. After enlisting British help, they had been expecting British ships to come to meet them. But when they got there, they found the city surrounded by Republican troops. The rebels tried to take the city but could not and were forced to retreat. Then they fell prey to Republican forces. They died in their thousands, suffering from hunger and disease."

"So the British were going to help?... But what happened to the British ships?" asked Tim.

"They did not arrive till it was too late...The final battle was at *Savenay*...The revolutionary forces were brutal...farms were destroyed, crops and forests burned and villages razed...residents of the *Vendée* ...even innocents...were killed...regardless of their age."

"I didn't realise there was such resistance to the revolution." Lesley shook her head, bemused. She picked up the bottle of rosé and went to pour more wine. I quickly put my hand over the top of the glass.

"Not for me thanks!"

She looked a little surprised but didn't persist. She simply shrugged and filled up her own glass.

Meanwhile Monsieur Lagard shook his head in response to her remark.

"Not exactly *Madame*. Napoleon Bonaparte 'ad great respect for the *Vendéen* people ...'e understood that their fight was not a struggle against the Revolution, but a fight for the preservation of their liberty and freedom for their religion. 'e proposed a solution...if the *Vendéens* would stop fighting and pay their taxes, the churches would be allowed to reopen. Napoleon who admired the *Vendéens*' stance restored full rights of worship to the church, not only in the *Vendée*, but in the 'ole of France...Bonaparte also exempted them from conscription. 'e gave them full indemnity, and 'elped the reconstruction of the department...To 'elp supervise the region, the capital was moved from *Fontenay* to *La Roche-sur-Yon*...this created the first Napoleonic town built on a grid system. This 'as been copied in many towns and cities in America."

"And the tunnels?" prompted Lesley.

Monsieur Lagard was so engrossed in his history lesson he had forgotten the reason he was telling us about the wars.

"Oh, of course...the tunnels." He cleared his throat and took a sip of wine. "The *Vendéen* fighters, known as 'whites' or 'brigands' 'ad the 'abit of returning 'ome after a battle to tend their land...They used these tunnels to return 'ome after fighting...You see the rebels used guerrilla tactics...they were supported by the insurgents' local knowledge and the good-will of the people."

"Were many people killed during these rebellions?" I asked.

"Many died." He replied sadly. "They say five 'undred thousand *Vendéens* out of a population of eight 'undred thousand died...Regular soldiers were also killed, repeatedly beaten by peasants who were unarmed. Of course, many more rebels were killed than government troops."

"That's a lot of people" remarked Tim.

"*Oui*. Each side were guilty of the most terrible atrocities."

"How awful!"

"*Oui Madame*. Over six thousand rebel prisoners were executed."

"Were they shot?" asked Tim, obviously wanting more gruesome details.

"Many were killed in what was called the "*national bath*". They were tied in groups and loaded onto barges which were then sunk in the *Loire*. Among them were four 'undred children. Not only the remaining rebels and the people who 'ad given them support, but the innocent as well."

The mood around the room quickly became very sombre. It was a disturbing part of the area's history. Monsieur Lagard had given us a lot of information to digest and my mind filled with the thought of the terrible suffering endured by the families in the area.

"Is there any residue of bad feeling?" asked Tim.

Monsieur Lagard gave him a puzzled look. Tim attempted to clarify.

"I was just thinking –it's not really that long ago –about two hundred years. Are people in this area content to forgive and forget the past?"

Monsieur Lagard sighed. "Sometimes people are not too 'appy with Parisians coming to the area. But..." 'e shrugged in his Gallic fashion, "who knows about their reasons?"

Perhaps this diplomatic response and the way he tried not to blame anyone as the main aggressors gave us a clue as to the reason he was the *Maire.* Lesley persisted in her request for information about the tunnel under the house.

"So are you saying men would fight then use the tunnels under the houses to get back to their own house and family?"

"*Oui.*" Monsieur Lagard nodded. "They were 'elped by local people to 'ide there. They used them to escape. To get them to other places."

"So the tunnel under this house will come out...where... d'you think?"

"Per'aps into the villages or 'amlets around *L'Absie.*"

"It's a shame we can't investigate further and go right into the tunnel to see where it comes out." Lesley looked around at us.

"I'm not coming with you on that one." I shuddered.

"It's too dangerous anyway," Tim looked at Lesley shaking his head. "The *geometre* said it could be ready to collapse."

"It is better to get it filled in I think" said Monsieur Lagard decisively. It seemed to put an end to our speculation and discussion.

Having sensed we'd exhausted the topic of the tunnels and aware that we'd all finished eating about forty minutes earlier, Tim began to clear away the dishes. He announced that there was sticky toffee pudding for dessert if anyone was interested. We all responded enthusiastically. Death and destruction forgotten.

"Mmm lovely!"

"Sounds good to me!" agreed Monsieur Lagard patting his stomach.

I wondered how he knew so much about the Vendéen wars. It wasn't something I'd heard of before.

"So Monsieur Lagard, you seem to be an authority on the history of the area. Is that just borne out of interest?"

"*Madame?*" He looked puzzled.

"Did you study local history, perhaps at college? Or is it something that you became interested in yourself? "

He became very serious. "This violent 'istory of the *Vendée* is not taught in schools *Madame*. It is something the Republican government prefer not to tell. Nevertheless, I 'ave looked into the 'istory of the area to find out about my ancestors."

"Oooh, I've always thought about doing that myself" cooed Lesley.

Monsieur Lagard's face was solemn.

Ignoring Lesley's remark, I continued.

"Did you find anything interesting?"

"*Oui Madame.*" He drew himself up in his seat. "I found that I am a direct descendant of *Francois du Brecot, Comte de la Rossemaquelein.* 'e was one of the generals of the Royalist *Vendéen* insurrection during the French Revolution. 'e was killed by a Republican soldier near *Bressuire.* 'e fell in battle on 4 June 1815."

"Nooo!" Lesley interjected.

Just then Tim returned pushing his trolley.

"What have I missed this time?" he protested putting a large jug of custard on the table. Monsieur Lagard's eyes lit up at seeing it. It wasn't the '*crème anglais*' he was used to.

I chortled at Tim's mock outrage. Lesley's mouth was still agape with amazement. I announced grandly.

"It turns out... we are in the presence of the aristocracy."

Tim stopped what he was doing and looked at me in surprise.

"Aristoc?..." He began.

I nodded toward Monsieur Lagard who sat with quiet dignity listening to his introduction.

"Monsieur Lagard is descended from a Count who was a general and led rebels into battle during the *Vendéen* war!"

"Good Lord!" He stood holding the dessert bowls and shaking his head slowly in disbelief. "I feel like I should bow or something!"

Lesley and I giggled. I pictured how absurd Tim would look if he dropped into a deep bow every time he came across Monsieur Lagard.

"But didn't the aristocracy have to flee the country or they would be executed?"

"That is right, of course *Monsieur*" began Monsieur Lagard "My ancestor's family were exiled for a while in England. They returned two generations later as simple merchants and 'id their past from the French authorities. Of course, nowadays it does not matter if they know or not. What can they do?" He shrugged again, smiling.

"That is quite amazing! And you haven't mentioned it before!" admonished Lesley.

"It is not something I talk about." He watched carefully as Tim dished out the sticky toffee pudding.

"People in the area know my background. They 'ave the pride that my ancestor fought with theirs and it is not a problem for them to 'ave me as *maire* who is also a descendant of aristocracy."

He helped himself to custard.

Despite his aristocratic ancestry and obvious pride in it, Monsieur Lagard seemed unperturbed by others reaction to it.

After finishing dessert Monsieur Lagard quizzed us on our knowledge about the emblem of the *Vendée* - two inter-linked hearts with a cross on top. I guessed, after what he'd told us, that the cross perhaps symbolized the church.

He looked pleased "That is right *Madame*! The twin love of the *Vendéens* for their country and the church."

I stifled a yawn just as Tim brought in the coffee. I was glad to have something to keep me awake a little longer. The concentration needed for Monsieur

Lagard's story had made me tired. It was approaching eleven and I felt it had been a long day.

While we had coffee we chatted generally about family, all of us recognising that the evening was drawing to an end. Monsieur Lagard had arranged a taxi, knowing that his son was otherwise engaged and therefore couldn't pick him up. It arrived on time at eleven on the dot. He thanked Lesley and Tim for the lovely food and good company and went on his way. I also said my farewells thanking them for a wonderful evening. Lesley and I reminded each other as I stepped out of their door, of the time for our trip out the following day.

Outside the air had cooled and it was dark. I was glad I had such a short distance to walk home. There was a light on the wall outside Lesley's front door which shone bright enough only to light the path directly outside her house. Luckily, the sky was cloud free and the moon was full which cast a silvery light across the gardens and helped to illuminate the whole route across to my house.

I noticed as I picked my way toward my front door that Mr Saleem's car was in the courtyard. Spotting a light on in the chambres d'hôtes, I glanced towards it and caught a glimpse of him standing at his window. In that brief moment I could see that he was looking out toward the courtyard and appeared to be on his phone. I couldn't be sure but it also seemed as if he moved hastily away from the window after noticing me. I put my head down immediately on seeing him do this, instantly regretting looking up and hoping he didn't think I was snooping.

Despite feeling tired, I didn't feel ready for sleep and decided to relax for a while on the terrace. I lit a couple of citronella candles in the hope of keeping insects away and sat with a warm woollen cardigan pulled around me, gazing out onto the moonlit garden and hills beyond. I thought about the history of the area as told by Monsieur Lagard. Or should I say *Comte Lagard?* I wondered if where I was sitting and the land I was looking out across had been where murder and mayhem had taken place from *Vendéen* battles which had spilt over into the *Deux Sevres*. I imagined the fear as families fought for their lives. It was a sobering thought, and one I decided I should not be dwelling upon. It was the past.

After sitting for about twenty minutes I decided it was time for bed and went to lock up. On turning out the lights I heard the outer door from the chambres d'hôtes close and wondered if it was Sophie returning. Then I heard a car start up and head off down the lane. I realised it sounded more like someone was leaving. I thought it strange at this time of night and wondered if it was Mr Saleem. Maybe something to do with his phone call. Well, if he wanted to go out at such a late hour that was his business. I headed upstairs to bed.

CHAPTER NINE

Saturday

I was up bright and early the next morning and made my usual journey to the bread van. Another warm day I suspected though the air was now becoming very close. There was a little more cloud cover than usual and I wondered briefly if rain was forecast later.

Walking past the courtyard I noticed Mr Saleem's car and wondered what time he'd returned during the night. If it had been Mr Saleem's car that I'd heard leaving. Goodness knows where he could have been going at such a late hour. It wasn't as if *L'Absie* had any thriving nightlife.

Sophie's car, I noted, was missing. I presumed she must have stayed out all night. Well Sophie was a grown woman and could do as she liked. It wasn't my business.

"*Bonjour Catareen!*" Marie looked bright as a button.

"*Bonjour Marie*" I approached the van and was about to ask whether she had recovered from the excessive amount of wine we had consumed a couple of days before, when she interrupted.

"'ave you 'eard?..." looking at the confusion on my face she realised I clearly hadn't.

"There was a terrible accident on the *rue du Niort* in the early 'ours of this morning."

The lane from our hamlet led onto the D744. It was also the main road into Niort, the nearest large town.

"How serious?...Anyone hurt?" I asked, concerned.

"Apparently they 'ad to cut someone out of the car...but there was only one car involved!"

This is why she looked so sprightly. She was obviously relishing being able to bring news, despite its depressing nature.

"Speeding d'you think?... drink driving and lost control of the car?..." I thought vaguely of scenarios whereby someone could crash a car yet no one else was involved.

"'Who knows?..." she shrugged then added "André was at the scene. Per'aps Sophie will find out about it later?" she flashed me a meaningful look.

"Maybe..." My tone was deliberately noncommittal.

I didn't want to inform Marie that Sophie hadn't yet returned from her evening out. It wasn't anyone else's business what she did in her private life and certainly not Marie's. But her words made me contemplate both Sophie and André's actions. Had André left Sophie at home so he could go to the scene of an accident while she waited for him to return? I sighed wistfully, telling myself to stop speculating on what other people got up to and bade a swift but amicable farewell to Marie.

I returned to the house loaded with the usual warm, fresh, crusty bread and croissants. Mr Saleem was seated for breakfast again around eight thirty. After serving breakfast with a brief greeting, I left him to it, returning to clear away his dishes only after observing that he'd left the table. As he made his way out of the room, my thoughts turned to how I'd inadvertently noticed him at his window the previous night. Of course I made no mention of it. I certainly didn't want to bring his attention to the fact in case he got the wrong impression – thinking I was actually going out of my way to watch him. I also recalled the sound of his car leaving the hamlet at such a late hour, but again, it was no business of mine what he got up to so made no mention of it.

As I piled the dishes and cutlery onto the tray I sensed that Mr Saleem had halted in the doorway. I glanced up at him, surprised to find that he was loitering, as if reluctant to leave. Assuming he wanted my attention, I paused and smiled, raising my eyebrows with a questioning look. Unexpectedly, as if he had all the time in the world, he leaned back nonchalantly against the door frame, his hands shoved casually into his trouser pockets and regarded me steadily. I waited for him to speak, feeling increasingly uncomfortable under his gaze while anxiously wondering whether he was about to accuse me of spying on him.

Suddenly, as if from nowhere he said.

"I went into *Luçon* yesterday."

Secretly relieved at the insignificance of the subject matter, my attention resumed to clearing dishes as I attempted to smile with a polite response.

"Oh that's nice."

His altercation with Sophie the previous day filled my mind and I struggled not to let his potentially unchivalrous behaviour colour my view of him, recalling the stony look that had been on his face and how she'd ignored his presence that same evening, then his departure late at night. I had no idea what it was all about but I was beginning to have serious misgivings about him.

He continued light-heartedly, regardless of my hopefully not obvious lack of interest. "I enjoyed walking around the old quarter... the cobbled streets are charming ...and the old buildings...there is a lot of history."

Though I was in no mood for small talk I didn't want to appear impolite so simply agreed that it was very pretty, while focussing on the task at hand, finally pulling the tray toward me as I prepared to lift it.

Sensing his reluctance to leave, with my hands holding onto the tray, I glanced up at him only to find that he was studying me rather intently. Apprehension took hold and I deliberately attempted to keep my tone light.

"So do you have plans for sight seeing today?"
He didn't reply immediately and an uncomfortable few moments passed as we traded looks. I felt increasingly unnerved by his stare but then attempted to hide my relief when he finally gave an unthreatening response.

"I am going into the village for a newspaper...I intend to spend some time relaxing... no rushing about today... just enjoying the beautiful views and spending some time alone."

He fell silent again and I nodded and smiled then looked down once again to pick up the tray.   Expecting him to make his exit, this being an obvious end to the conversation, I saw out of the corner of my eye that he still didn't make any attempt to leave. I hesitated, not wanting to turn my back on him to return to the kitchen in case he wanted to say more. At last he spoke.

"So I will see you later" His tone was flat and he was waiting, clearly expecting a response.

Forcing a smile I opened my mouth to return his sentiment but without giving me the chance, he abruptly turned away, as if suddenly making up his mind about something and needing to leave in that instant. I stared at the doorway openmouthed at his lack of courtesy and reproached myself for not waiting until he was long gone before retrieving the dishes.

Eventually carrying the tray into the kitchen while disconcerted with his manner, I placed it hastily on the counter top and instantly gave in to my uneasiness by returning immediately to lock the adjoining door between the chambres d'hôtes and our kitchen. Then, leaning back against the door and breathing a heavy sigh of relief, I considered what Karl's reaction would be. *There's nowt so queer as folk* he would probably say and consider my behaviour to be an overreaction. Deciding he would no doubt be right, I made a great effort at shrugging off the encounter and putting it from my mind.

*

It was exactly ten thirty when Lesley showed up. She was early but I was ready to go.

"Ready?"

"As I'll ever be."

I followed her out, locking the outer door.

If I'd been forewarned and a religious person, I would have said a prayer before getting into the car with Lesley. This was my first time as her passenger and it soon became obvious that she was somewhat flippant about the rules of the road. Frequently forgetting that she was supposed to drive on the right, not on the left as in the UK, was a particular problem at roundabouts.

Pointing to the technology set up on the dashboard she said.

"I've put the location into the sat nav and it is *usually* accurate so we should be okay finding it"

"Right" I replied, not entirely convinced.

"Just one other thing..."

"Mmm?..."

Lesley was looking a bit sheepish.

"It's in French cos' I use it to help me improve so sometimes I'm not sure whether I understand the directions correctly..."

I looked at her incredulously.

Seeing my look she began to protest "Well...you speak better French so we should be okay!"

"Right." I repeated slowly. Though I was flattered by the faith she had in my linguistic skills I couldn't help but be amused. It was just like Lesley. She couldn't use a CD in her home to practise her French like everyone else.

Although not wanting to take my eyes of the road, I took the chance to glance down at the information I'd printed out from a tourist website. I read it aloud.

"Situated in the village of *Louresse-Rochemenier*, six kilometres north west of *Doué-la-Fontaine,* just off the D761"

"That's right."

"So according to this..." I glanced up at the road, relieved that we were still on the right hand side.

"...It's slightly off the beaten track..." I carried on reading. "This most unusual museum is worth a visit...blah, blah, blah...reveals a community of two ancient farms and their associated dwellings...carved out of the local stone in a quarry type setting. It is possible to visit all manner of different properties...fully furnished...giving an insight into a totally unique way of life...barns...wine cellar...communal village oven..."

"Mmm, wonder how that worked?" Lesley said vaguely, as if to herself.

I continued reading aloud, ignoring her question "...stables and underground church to visit. Guided tours available, in English, or feel free to wander around at your own pace." I looked up at her. "You bothered about a guided tour?"

"No, not really."

"Me neither. We'll just wander." I paused. Looking ahead I saw another roundabout looming. There were no other cars about so I didn't feel too anxious about Lesley's driving around this one.

I glanced down again to put the sheet of paper back into my bag when I felt the car lurch. In a panic I seized hold of the door handle to steady myself.

"Hey!" shouted Lesley angrily.

Looking up I saw a car speeding off ahead into the distance. A silver car. Lesley was furious.

"He nearly pushed me off the road! I was in the right lane! Who does he think he is?" I shook my head, sympathising with her sentiment as she raged for several minutes about his lousy driving skills. She then went on to rant about how men blamed woman for poor driving when if fact she believed men were worse. I simply nodded in agreement, not wanting to become involved in any kind of debate while she was supposed

to be watching the road. When she eventually fell silent I thought of the incident with the idiot driver from a few days earlier, still baffled about where on earth he'd come from. How had he been behind my car after I left Di's house when there were no other houses in that area and the road itself was a dead end? Recalling feeling similar outrage, I attempted a conciliatory tone.

"Some drivers have no consideration for others."

She didn't respond and we both fell silent for several minutes as she tried to shake off the incident. Observing after a while that Lesley was still silently seething, I attempted to alleviate her mood with mundane comments about the surrounding landscape. The distraction was effective. Toward the latter part of the journey, Lesley became much calmer and we reached our destination without further mishap.

Our approach to the village was a steep descent on a narrow bank between two huge walls of rock. I was instantly relieved that Lesley was wise enough to slow the car to a virtual snail's pace to prevent it from careering downhill.

Parking areas were clearly signposted so we followed the signs and parked in the nearest spot we could find outside a medieval church.

The village was known for its troglodyte caves and I was keen to survey the steep walls of rock surrounding us in an attempt to catch glimpses of life in the tiny openings of the rock face. To get our bearings, we scanned our surroundings as soon as we emerged from the car and found to our delight that above and behind the houses and buildings in the centre of the village, it was possible to make out houses in the rock face. Potted plants sat on steps carved into the rock next to coloured wooden front doors. The rock also seemed to be adorned with beautiful multi-coloured plants which cascaded down the walls. Because of their distance, the dwellings appeared in miniature, like enchanted faery houses.

It was the nearby underground church that had sparked my interest on the tourist website and we quickly found there were plenty of signs to indicate directions for places of interest. As it was nearly eleven thirty, we decided to investigate the area first then find a café later for lunch or at least a snack.

Initially we believed the village itself to be fairly deserted, perhaps because it was early in the tourist season. Then, after following the sign for the underground church we were surprised to find a group of a dozen or so people being ushered together for the beginning of a tour. The woman leading the tour was French but speaking in English. She saw us approach and asked if we wanted to join in the group. It was okay by me so I glanced at Lesley to gauge her reaction.

"Fine with me," she shrugged.

The tour guide acknowledged our response and informed us we could pay the entrance fee later as she was keen to get the tour started on time.

We shuffled along behind the crowd toward the underground entrance. Listening to the chattering voices in the group, I deduced we were tagging along with a group of Dutch tourists. Lowering my voice I said, "that was fortunate, especially as she's speaking in English."

"Yes, great timing." Lesley paused "Oh-oh, this looks a bit scary."

A few yards ahead there was a wide and low entrance carved out of the rock face. I heard the tour guide tell us to watch our heads as we entered.

Although I had to stoop a little at the entrance, the low passage quickly opened out into a large room with a much higher, vaulted ceiling. The air was cooler than outside but not unpleasantly so. The rocky walls were whitewashed in places and there were al fresco paintings on the walls, all of a religious nature. The tour guide ushered us all into one place toward the altar and began her spiel about the history of the place. I didn't listen too closely to what was being said as I preferred to let the history wash over me by simply soaking up the atmosphere. Gazing around at the paintings, I marvelled at the detail and was amazed that many of the rich colours had not faded with time.

Over to the right hand side behind the tour guide was a large statue of Mary. The tour guide gestured as she spoke, toward the large golden crucifix on the wall behind the statue. I noticed Lesley taking a lot of interest in what she was saying and I stepped back from the group slightly to look around, noting the seating in the room. About a dozen long wooden benches, which looked fairly uncomfortable if you had to sit on them for any length of time, stretched from one side of room to the other behind us. I wondered if they were in place for parishioners with the church still in use today or maybe just for visitors such as ourselves. After all the huge medieval church in the centre of the village still seemed like it was still in regular use.

Intending to revert my attention to the words of the tour guide, I swung round toward her just as I caught a movement in my peripheral vision. I glanced toward the passageway from where we had just come and for a split second I had the sensation that someone was lurking in the shadows. I leaned slightly forward, craning my head to get a better look and noticed the outline of a shadow suddenly shrink. I took a step forward trying to peer into darkness but could not see anyone.

Feeling a little uncomfortable at the possibility of someone loitering in the passageway who didn't want to be seen, I moved closer to the group. Safety in numbers I mused. Once I was near the others I was unable to resist. I glanced back toward the passageway. Nothing. Maybe my mind was playing tricks.

Because Lesley was so enthralled with the tour guide's information we stayed with the group for the whole time she was talking inside the church. Once we were out in the sunlight again we decided not to carry on with the rest of the tour preferring to check out the village ourselves. We went to pay the tour guide our six euros for the tour while she chatted to people who were asking questions about the church. Lesley thanked her profusely and said how she'd found the historical information fascinating. We then excused ourselves from the group by telling the guide we had been before – we hadn't – but had only missed the church visit. She looked a little disappointed that we wanted to part company but didn't press us further.

"I noticed a café just to the right of where we're parked. We could go for a drink before doing anything else" suggested Lesley.

"Yes. That'll be nice." I toyed with the idea of telling her about seeing someone skulking around behind us in the church but decided against it. I had probably imagined it anyway.

As we turned the corner toward the café we found that the Dutch crowd had had the same idea. The café had become very busy all of a sudden.

I groaned. "They must have found a more direct route."

"We'll be lucky to get a seat" agreed Lesley with a grimace.

As we drew near, we scanned the place for empty tables and were surprisingly fortunate to find one. Entering the café through the gap in the wall marked exit rather than entrance, we hastened to put our bags down onto one of the tables to lay claim to it. It was at that point we noticed a few of the Dutch people in one corner looking over the small stone wall surrounding the café. They were pointing at something and it looked like they were discussing something with the waiter. Curiosity getting the better of us, we both moved toward the group to peer over the same part of the wall. There was about a six foot drop on the other side and a tap sticking out of one of the rocky walls opposite. Steps led up to the tap.

"Looks like a natural spring," observed Lesley.

"Mmm, that must be nice, to get fresh, clean water straight from the land."

Curiosity satisfied, we returned to our table and picked up the menus which had been left there. Lesley picked up her bag to place it underneath. I searched around for my bag as I was sure I'd also left it on the table. Lesley saw my puzzled look.

"What's wrong?"

"I left my bag here. It seems to have disappeared." She joined in the search as we simultaneously scoured the area around and underneath the table. I thought immediately of the worst case scenario. Lesley caught my look and guessed my thoughts.

"Anything of value in it?"

I thought carefully. "Just purse...about sixty euros...and keys...apart from that a few pens, lipstick...tissues." I remembered that my diary which revealed my address, was in my other bag and still in my car. I hadn't got around to swapping everything across when I'd changed bags a few days earlier. Di's scarf was also still in my other bag.

"Phone?"

"No, I think I took it out in your car when I was looking at the website information for this place. I'm pretty sure I put it on the shelf underneath the glove box and I think I've left it there"

"Oh well then. If someone's got it they haven't got away with much."

Maybe not, but not having my keys was going to be a major inconvenience.

Just then a waiter appeared at the table.

"Are you looking for something *Madame*?" He was carrying my bag.

"Yes" I smiled at him, relieved. I took the bag. "Thank you so much. Where did you find it?"

He gestured toward the entrance.

"It was found by a lady over there."

"Oh." I turned to give Lesley a puzzled look.

The waiter began to move away, clearly not wanting to waste time since it was a such a busy period.

"Thank you again." I called to the waiter but he was already on his way.

Lesley glanced around surreptitiously at the people sitting at the tables nearby and lowered her voice to a near whisper.

"We haven't been anywhere near there."

"I know." I replied lowering my voice in the same manner.

I looked inside my bag.

"Check to see if everything's there" urged Lesley as I did so.

I rummaged through the contents. Everything was still there. I checked my purse and found the money was also there. Surprised, I opened the purse wide to show Lesley.

"That's strange." She paused. "Why would anyone take your bag then leave the money?"

We both went quiet. I shrugged and shook my head.

"It's very odd... But oh well" I sighed, "all's well that ends well."

Lesley let out a sigh but nodded in agreement. We said no more about it. Though I sensed it was still in our thoughts for a while afterwards because we both sat quietly, a little subdued in fact, until our food arrived about ten minutes later.

We left the café, mostly back to our normal selves, having each consumed a *croque monsieur* and coffee. As we strolled between the houses along the narrow cobbled streets, we frequently glanced up toward the rocky backdrop in the hope of catching a glimpse of the people living there. And we did a couple of times. It struck me as strange seeing grown people living in the rock and it still made me feel as if I was expecting some kind of faery folk to come darting out of one of the openings.

Heading back to the car a little before two we both expressed enjoyment at what a pleasant trip this had been in spite of 'the incident'.

As Lesley steered to reverse the car out of the parking space I noticed a silver car parked opposite. As the other car also began to reverse, Lesley peered over her shoulder to get a better look.

"Did you see what type of car it was that passed us on the road?"

I shook my head, "just that it was silver."

"Mmm…" Lesley was now looking pointedly at the car opposite.

There was really no reason to believe this was the car that had caused Lesley so much consternation. The paranoia was obviously catching. That being said, as we left the village I still took the time to peer closely into the wing mirror to get a side view of the road behind. Nothing.

The uneasy feeling abated as we chatted amiably on the return journey about various everyday things as well as Lesley's impending visit from her family.

Despite gradually feeling able to relax while Lesley was driving, I still felt a wave of relief as she turned the corner into our hamlet.

Relief immediately turned to horror as the car suddenly swerved violently to one side and with a jolt came to a grinding halt. We now had an extremely close up view of brambles pressed forcibly against the windscreen. In the split second we'd been jerked forward in our seats as the car lunged, I'd managed to catch a glimpse of the object Lesley had swerved narrowly to miss. *A silver car.* I was fairly sure it was larger than Mr Saleem's. Already moving rapidly away from us, we heard it skid as it turned to get out of the hamlet onto the main road. I looked back at Lesley. Her face was white with shock.

"You okay?"

She nodded slowly, her voice trembling "Just about..."

"He didn't stop!"

She looked at me aghast *"He could've killed us!"*

I nodded, not wanting to dwell on that thought.

"Can you reverse to get us out? Or do you want me to drive?"

Lesley looked at the steering wheel and dashboard like she'd never seen them before. Her hands were shaking.

"No...no...I'll be okay." I wasn't convinced but knew she only had to move the car a hundred yards or so to get to the house so decided I could trust her to make it that far.

Lesley breathed a heavy sigh in an attempt to pull herself together and then put the car into reverse.

"Don't they say that you should get back behind the steering wheel as soon as you can if you have an accident?" she laughed nervously "You know, so you don't lose your nerve?"

I nodded reassuringly "I think so..." though I thought it was usually said about riding a bike, or falling off a horse, or something like that. I didn't think it was the time or place to discuss it.

Lesley pulled the car back onto the road and I wondered how badly the paintwork would be scratched from the brambles while at the same time being relieved to have made it home alive.

CHAPTER TEN

Not long after we returned home and still feeling a little shaken, I had an unexpected visit from Monsieur Lagard. He brought me the distressing news that Sophie had been in a car accident.

"*What? How?*" I asked, shocked

Immediately I considered the possibility that it could be the car crash Marie had mentioned that morning. Deep in thought, I made no comment about his news and remained silent for several moments. At long last I found Monsieur Lagard was studying my face with a concerned look.

"Are you alright *Madame*?"

I regarded him blankly realising that both the incident in Lesley's car and hearing about Sophie's crash so soon afterwards was making me feel rather queasy. Taking a deep breath to steady myself I shrugged off my own discomfort to focus on what had happened to Sophie. I offered a weak smile.

."How is she? ...Is she? ..." Dreading the worst, I was reluctant to voice my thoughts.

"*Non, Madame.*" He shook his head. "Miraculously...she is going to be alright." He patted my arm sympathetically. "She 'as a broken rib and a few cuts and bruises...of course, she is very shook up...but the doctors 'ave said she will be okay."

He told me that she had left her date with André at around twelve thirty in the morning to return to her room here at the chambres d'hôtes. He stipulated that she had *not* been drinking - before I'd even had the chance to ask. André had received a phone call at about two am, informing him that he was needed at the scene of a car accident. Another driver had seen the car overturn and had had the wherewithal to call the emergency services immediately. André had arrived at about the same time as an ambulance and he had helped to cut the driver out of the car. He was, according to his father, very upset when he realised who the driver was. Sophie had then been taken to hospital in Parthenay.

I let out a sigh of relief. "Thank God she's okay." My thoughts went straight to her family. They must be informed and said as much to Monsieur Lagard.

"Of course, *Madame*..." he nodded in agreement "I will leave that up to you...but for now the doctors say she needs a lot of rest. They say they are willing to let 'er out of 'ospital, perhaps tomorrow, but only if she 'as someone to give 'er total care for the next few days"

"Oh I see." I deliberated for a moment. I only had Mr Saleem as a guest so it was feasible that I could look after her.

"I could..." I began.

He had already guessed my response and interrupted gently.

"Do not worry, *Madame*... André is at the 'ospital with 'er, as 'e has been all night..." He paused to let this information sink in. "'e has offered 'er 'is 'ome for 'er to recover...'e told me that 'e 'as already made arrangements to look after 'er"

"That's very kind of him." I was moved by his compassion.

"Not *kind Madame*." He smiled knowingly, "Per'aps *love*, eh?"

He looked pleased. So Marie was right. He was keen for André to settle down. Well Sophie would make a wonderful daughter in law. My God, I thought, even I was marrying her off! And they had only known each other for such a short time!

I thanked Monsieur Lagard for bringing me the news and said that I would make sure I informed the magazine Sophie worked for so they could pass the information on to her family. He assured me that he would give Sophie my kindest regards and wishes for a speedy recovery.

"Per'aps you could arrange to visit Sophie at Andrés 'ouse?" he suggested. I had started to think about visiting her in the hospital, but maybe he was right. It would give her time to rest.

"Of course...I could visit tomorrow when she gets there. And I'll have her bags ready as soon as she needs them."

He nodded, satisfied. "Thank you *Madame*...I will tell André to call in 'ere tomorrow for 'er things" and then added as an afterthought " 'e can give you directions to 'is 'ouse."

After wishing me *bonne journée,* he left.

Despite knowing that Sophie was alright, I found the news very disturbing. For some time I stood by the kitchen sink, staring without focus of the window, just contemplating our fragile mortality. Reflecting on recent events, I shook my head in disbelief. There I was thinking Sophie had stayed out all night enjoying herself when in fact she'd been nearly killed. Thank God someone had seen her car overturn otherwise she might still be there. *At what time did he say? Two o'clock in the morning?* But didn't he also say she'd left Andre's house at twelve thirty? Was he mistaken? If not, where had she been for an hour and a half? It was only a five minute trip in the car to the village where André lived. Unless the accident happened earlier and she was only discovered at two. But didn't someone see what had happened and phone for an ambulance straightaway? Surely it didn't take them over an hour to get there? André would be able to get there in only a few minutes. *So what was the time delay?* Monsieur Lagard must be mistaken about the time. There was no other explanation.

Eventually, shaking my head with the thought that things could have been much worse, I breathed a heavy sigh of relief. Then, with a concerted effort, I pulled myself together and purposefully set off to Sophie's room. I wanted to make sure her belongings were ready to pick up in case André came for them sooner rather than later. I also knew Mr Saleem was out. So to kill two birds with one stone, I decided to quickly make up his room while I was there.

Unfortunately my timing wasn't good. On leaving Sophie's room I came face to face with Mr Saleem. His hand was on the door handle to his room as if he was just about to enter. He glanced at the suitcase in my hand quizzically.

"Is the young lady leaving?" The question seemed innocent enough.

"She's been in an accident."

He frowned "Not serious I hope."

"No, thankfully."

Irritation flashed across his face. Was he expecting a full run down? I continued.

"A few cuts and bruises but she'll be okay."

He made no response so assuming he didn't want to add anything further, I turned my back on him to lock the door to Sophie's room.

"Please send her my good wishes...in hospital?" I turned toward him again and found him looking at me expectantly. His manner, as before at breakfast, was making me feel ill at ease. Yet I just couldn't put my finger on the reason why.

Instinctively, I felt reluctant to tell him where she was so I lied.

"For now...but...er ...I'm not sure after that."

"I see..." he studied my face.

The landing where we stood facing each other was such a confined space, I was beginning to feel hemmed in. Was there a change in his manner? Or was that simply paranoia on my part?

I looked away. "Anyway, I have such a lot to do" another lie as I forced a light tone. "I'll see you later." Without waiting for a reply, I moved to squeeze past him. He swiftly stepped aside and I scurried off toward the stairs.

Back in the safety of the kitchen I reflected on what had just happened. I was beginning to think there was something distinctly odd in the way he had been looking at me. When I first saw him, I'd thought him charming...but now...he was starting to give me the creeps. Once again I brought to mind his encounter with Sophie a few days earlier. She'd looked troubled after speaking to him. Had he said something to her which was inappropriate? And why did he want to know where she was? Was he going to visit the poor girl in hospital to harass her? Reproaching myself for letting my imagination run riot, I wished Karl was back. He was the voice of reason. He would probably advise me to stop second guessing other people's motives when their actions were probably perfectly innocent.

*

As I placed Sophie's suitcase under the stairs my stomach rumbled and I became acutely aware that I had not eaten since my lunchtime snack. It was now a little after five so I went to prepare a sandwich and brew some coffee.

A short while later I was sitting at the kitchen table drinking my second cup of coffee and just enjoying the moment of dunking a ginger biscuit when I had an unexpected visit from Di.

"Hi!" She called, popping her head round the door.

I looked up in surprise.

"I saw you sitting there through the kitchen window so thought I'd come straight in." Her face looked strained and I suspected there was something amiss.

"Yes, of course...come in" I immediately got up to give her a hug, feeling not only pleased to see her but very glad of the company. While she sank down heavily on a chair at the table, I went to fetch another cup, hoping there was just enough coffee left in the pot. Di breathed a deep sigh, put both elbows on the table and pushed her hair back with an air of exasperation.

"What a day!" she exclaimed.

Now what?

"Tell me all."

I sat down opposite and pushed the biscuits towards her. I was fed and watered and could now cope with whatever else the day brought me.

"Well...I've just been towed to a garage in *Secondigny* for a new tyre because I had a blow out would you believe on the way back from *Niort*." She shook her head, blinking back tears. "I had to wait an hour for the tow truck."

"Oh no!" I said sympathetically, putting my hand on her arm. Surely it can't have been that much of an ordeal to have her in this state of distress.

"That's not all of it." She continued. "I've been up most of the night worrying about whether I was going mad!"

"Huh?" I looked at her, confused.

She looked directly at me, her voice raised in agitation.

"I am *sure* someone was prowling around outside in the garden last night."

"Really?..did you phone the police?"

"Oh yes." She laughed bitterly. "They...two local *gendarmes*...didn't find anybody....and made me feel about this big." She raised her hand showing thumb and forefinger close together to emphasise her point. I instantly thought about the insane driver who for reasons known only to himself, had been close to Di's house. I decided it was better not to tell her about the incident – it would only cause her more anxiety.

"Did you let Jess out?" I didn't think Jess, her old golden Labrador, would be able to fend off intruders but she might have scared them off with her bark. Di had had the same idea.

"It was the first thing I did...I thought if they heard a dog bark, they might scarper...but even after she came back in the house...I was sure there was still someone out there." She shook her head wearily.

"Needless to say, I didn't get a wink of sleep...just kept wondering whether I was going to be murdered in my bed...and a fat load of good the police were." She snorted.

"Did you have a look this morning?...You know...to see if there was any sign anyone had been there?"

"Yes, but...there wasn't anything..." She sighed resignedly. "Oh, maybe I was mistaken and it was just shadows...like the police said." She spat out this last part.

"Mmm...what about tonight?" I asked "Will you be okay on your own?"

Di's house was too remote for my liking. Although our house was off the beaten track somewhat we still had three lots of neighbours we could hopefully count on if there was an emergency.

"Yes...I think so..." She shook her head as if to clear it. "I need to stop being so paranoid" Join the club, I thought.

"Anyway," she added with a defiant look, "Phil has a gun in the attic and he's shown me how to use it, so I've decided to put it under the bed - just in case."

I stared at her aghast. I couldn't even contemplate using a gun. Just as well I suppose because I didn't know how.

"*God, Di....be careful.*" I warned "It might be just kids messing about...you don't want to end up in prison for murder."

"Oh I think I'd only use it if I felt threatened in the house..." She assured me. "I wouldn't go shooting at things outside."

"*Thank God!*"

All the same I wasn't so sure it was a good idea to even have the gun in the house. But I didn't say any more about it and changed the subject in the hope that she would calm down a little. I told her about the tunnel under Lesley's house and how they needed to fill it up so the house wouldn't fall down. That sparked her interest. I was undecided about whether to tell her about Sophie. It was bad news and I wanted to keep the tone of the conversation light but she pre-empted me by asking how the reporter was getting on so I divulged what I knew about the accident.

"*Jesus!* Had she been drinking?"

"Apparently not, according to Monsieur Lagard."

She shook her head in disbelief.

"Are you going to visit her in hospital?"

"I thought about it but Monsieur Lagard reckons she'll be at André's house by tomorrow so I'll visit her there."

"Mmm...it would also give the two love birds some time alone," she mused raising her eyebrows.

By the time we strolled out toward her car, Di seemed to be back to her usual self. Opening the car door she said.

"It's so warm...isn't it odd?"

I nodded toward the sky above the house.

"Looks like rain clouds coming over so if we have a downpour I suppose it might cool down a little."

"Yes, I suppose we shouldn't complain." She remarked drily.

I suddenly remembered Di's scarf. It was still in the bag in the boot of my car. I knew the car was open and went to get it.

"Not as if you'll need it today, of course." I passed it to her.

"God, no..." She paused to think as she draped it carelessly over one shoulder.

"I forgot to tell you about my client." Her face became suddenly animated. "He wants a portrait painting of his granddaughter for her birthday."

"*And?...*" I knew she'd done work like this before but the look on her face meant there was something more.

"*And...*he is none other than the *cousin* of one of the leading politicians in the government...though he didn't specify who it was."

"Woah!...friends in high places...maybe he'll pass on some gossip about him – or her." I grinned mischievously.

Di glanced behind me toward the chambres d'hôtes just as I caught sight of Mr Saleem's appearance at the entrance. Thankfully Di dismissed his presence and carried on talking. I was glad. I certainly didn't feel like making introductions.

"I'll see him on Tuesday so will let you know if I find out anything."

We hugged briefly then she climbed into her car. The radio came on as she turned on the engine and lowered the window. I raised my voice slightly to be heard over it.

"Well, take care and..." I squeezed her arm "...don't worry!"

I didn't want to jog her memory about her restless night but I'd felt compelled to say something to allay her fears. She grimaced.

"Okay, see you later!"

I watched her drive off then turned back toward the house. Mr Saleem had retreated back into the chambres d'hôtes even though he had just a few minutes earlier looked as if he was on his way out. Perhaps he'd been loitering in an attempt to speak to me then had given up. Oh well, I'd had a narrow escape. Though I was certainly starting to wonder about his coming and goings. Knowing he was only going to be there one more day meant I could easily make myself scarce and avoid further awkward encounters. I calculated that I could ensure the dishes on Sunday from his final breakfast remained on the table until he'd left the dining room completely, then I could clear up without having to converse with him at all. If only there were more guests for him to chat to I might not be having this problem, I thought ruefully. But then again, maybe it's a good thing there weren't any. If he'd upset Sophie he might have upset others. I sighed miserably, hoping I would soon have more guests. That way I wouldn't have time to dwell on the peculiarities of other people.

This inner dialogue reminded me that I needed to check the website for enquiries and see if there'd been any phone messages left.

I cursed when soon after I realised I'd missed another call from Karl. I listened with a smile to his voice on the machine and was tempted to return his call straightaway but he said that he and Aidan would be at the convention for most of the day so advised me not to bother phoning back. He also gave me the troubling news that Aidan thought it likely the website had been hacked and sabotaged. I stared at the machine in disbelief as Karl explained the reasoning behind Aidan's theory of how malicious code had been used to infiltrate the site. He went on to say that he was sceptical about the sabotage idea because he thought it was such an odd thing to do. He finished by informing me that Aidan was going to work on it over the next few days to get it up and running again and would be in touch on Sunday evening around seven to let me know the details of his return flight.

There were no other messages. There were no emails from potential guests. And if Aidan's suspicions were correct, I might have the reason why. Sabotage was difficult to believe. It also didn't explain why I'd had guests cancelling just days prior their arrival.

For a few moments I pondered the strange events of the last few days. A maniac driver who tried to intimidate and run me off the road before turning up to stare me out at the fête. Could it be the same driver that forced Lesley to suddenly veer off road into the bushes? And what about a sabotaged website? Not so sure I believed that one. Di thought she'd had an intruder. Could it be the same man? If so for what reason? And what about the person in the underground church? Was there someone really there or was it my imagination? And my bag? How did my bag disappear and reappear somewhere I hadn't been with everything still intact? This last incident seemed so insignificant yet put together with other strange events made me wonder...

Unable to make sense of it I committed myself to dealing with everyday household chores to take my mind off things. Remaining in the house meant I was also less likely to encounter Mr Saleem.

The weather was becoming muggy. I was sure we'd soon have a downpour and so interrupted sweeping up in the kitchen to step outside and gauge the likelihood of rain. The air was heavy. I scanned the sky overhead and saw that there was now a lot of dark, grey cloud which was dense and low. A woman's laughter emanating from somewhere across the lane caught my attention. I looked across toward Lesley's house to see that she was in her garden having what appeared to be a very friendly *tête à tête* across a hedgerow with Mr Saleem. By her frequent laughter and body language I took it that she was greatly enamoured by his conversation. Doubt crept in. Could I be mistaken about him? Maybe the events of the last few days had taken their toll and I was becoming sensitive about the slightest thing. I had believed him to be very charming initially and after observing the two of them surreptitiously for several minutes, I concluded that he was obviously working his magic on Lesley. Part way through this charm offensive, Mr Saleem unexpectedly turned to gesture towards the house. Not wanting to be spotted, I made a hasty retreat into the hallway, hoping they hadn't caught me spying.

*

As the evening drew in, I checked the weather report on t.v. If the weather didn't break soon, I would have to begin watering the plants myself since many of them had flowered early and had begun to droop in the heat.

I flicked through the channels catching the tail end of the news a couple of times and then waited for the forecast. Eventually I learned that there was rain in the east but no break in the weather in the south west expected till Tuesday.

I turned off the television at about ten thirty and went to bed.

CHAPTER ELEVEN

Sunday

I didn't have the usual trek to the bread van on Sundays. It was Marie's day off. Now *baguettes*, as most people know, can be used to knock nails in after being kept for longer than a day, so Sunday's breakfasts were usually a selection of home baked *croissants*, toast and *brioche*.

Today being Mr Saleem's last day, I was determined to be in and out of the dining area with breakfast before he got a chance to engage me in conversation. I needn't have worried. On entering the room he bade me a curt good morning and told me quite matter of factly that after breakfast he would be walking up to the village and on his return would check out after settling his bill. I instinctively felt obliged to warn him about the impending downpour after having seen an ominous bank of dark clouds on the horizon but didn't want to engage in any further conversation so I thanked him for keeping me informed and in the same brisk like manner enquired whether he would like tea or coffee before returning to the kitchen.

When I returned with breakfast he remained silent as if preoccupied with his thoughts. His unwillingness to make idle chat suited me just fine so I left him to eat in peace. After making sharp work of breakfast he just as quickly made himself scarce. I reflected again on his manner while doing the dishes but was unable to fathom the change in him. The day before I had seen him turn on the charm for Lesley; a charm that I'd fallen for when we'd first met. I'd thought he was a pleasant and affable man but now I simply felt uneasy in his presence. My mind still kept going back to his encounter with Sophie.

Once the dishes had been washed I resolved to shake off this focus (or was it obsession?) with a guest I barely knew and would probably never see again and make another attempt at some rudimentary repair work on the hall door lock.

I was engrossed in this activity when I instinctively glanced up to find a tall, strapping *gendarme* of around thirty striding purposefully across the garden in my direction. He was dressed in the regulatory blue uniform, which I assumed must have been fairly uncomfortable to wear in the oppressive atmosphere. He also wore the standard issue calf length boots I'd seen on traffic police who stood by the side of the road with their motorcycles, speaking to harassed looking motorists. Looking every part the official guardian of the law with his gun holstered on his belt, I viewed him warily with involuntary feelings of guilt despite having done nothing illicit. Coming to a stop a few paces away, his large brown eyes regarded me coolly.

"*Madame* Patterson?" His tone was brisk and to the point.

I nodded "*Oui?*"

He announced, in impeccable English, that he had come to inform me that the authorities were investigating the car crash involving one of my guests. He explained that they were still trying to determine the cause of the accident.

"Oh?" He was obviously referring to Sophie's crash but I was still unsure about the purpose of his visit. Why did he need to let me know about this? Surely the investigation was normal procedure.

Seeing my look of confusion, he began to explain.

"The circumstances surrounding the crash are suspicious." He paused for a moment to let this sink in.

"Our initial investigations show that the brake cable 'ad been cut."

I was stunned. My mind whirled with the implication of his words.

"What?...Why on earth would someone want to do that?"

The *gendarme* was quiet for a moment and took off the kepi, his flat, circular peaked cap, showing a mop of curly, mousy brown hair. Stepping back a few paces, he moved away from the front door to scan the surroundings, looking across the now dry, thirsty garden toward the pool. He remained silent, his face impassive.

"*Why?*" I repeated, becoming anxious at his lack of response.

He turned to look across to Lesley's house and scratched his head with one hand while holding on to his hat with the other, obviously in no hurry to answer. I wondered whether he was using the silent treatment to intimidate or was he actually thinking carefully about his words. Either way, I was becoming impatient with his manner.

"That is why I am 'ere *Madame* Patterson" he said at last turning toward me and studying my face. I said nothing, just returned his blank look.

"I am trying to find out if..."

He pulled out a notebook from the top left pocket of his shirt and studied it.

"...*Mademoiselle* Shakil, 'ad any enemies. Perhaps she 'ad spoken to you about any problems she was 'aving?"

"Problems?...I've only known her a short time...I don't know her well enough to know about that. I presume you already know the reason she was staying here?"

He gazed at his notebook again.

"Er...to write something for a magazine?... Nothing more?" Answering my question with a question, he looked at me expectantly.

"I don't know of anything else" I replied honestly, seriously doubting whether there was anything else.

"You 'ave other guests 'ere?" he gestured toward the house.

"Just one, Mr Saleem. He'll be leaving today"

"Could I speak to 'im? Is 'e 'ere?"

He walked toward the end of the house and peered round the corner at the cars in the courtyard. My old Citroen and Mr Saleem's silver Saab were parked alongside each other.

" 'Fraid not. Mr Saleem, has gone up to the village and he hasn't returned yet."

"Okay." he looked at his watch, "I will come back later to speak to 'im." He replaced the notebook in his pocket "Thank you for your 'elp *Madame*."

He put on the kepi he was still holding and turned to go. He had parked his car in the lane outside of Lesley's house. I waited and watched as he got into his car then reversed it into the courtyard. Instead of moving off straightaway he paused a few moments, craning his neck to have a closer look at both cars. Ever vigilant, I thought, though I wondered what it was he was interested in. Then, without a backward glance, he drove off down the lane.

I was left feeling perplexed. Why would someone want to physically harm Sophie? She seemed such a gentle character. I shook my head, unable to understand any of it.

Di came to mind. In light of this recent information, I decided it was imperative to phone and check she was okay. Though I felt it was inconceivable that there could be any connection between this incident and Di's intruder, I decided it was better not to provide her with any details which would cause her further consternation.

Di's voice on answering the phone sounded upbeat. No, she said, she hadn't had any problems the previous night and had had a good night's sleep.

"Great!" Feeling both relieved and irritated with myself for even contemplating that there could be a problem. "Just thought I'd better check up on you."

"Thanks," she sounded grateful "But I'm okay. You were probably right about it being just kids."

"Ok, then I'll see you later."

I put the receiver down onto its cradle absent mindedly. Though I felt reassured about Di, the suspicions about Sophie's car nagged at me. Could the police be wrong? The officer had said *initial* investigation. So they hadn't completed it yet. Maybe when they do they'll realise their mistake. Of course, Sophie had said she wanted to tell me something before she'd gone for her date with André on Friday night. She had sounded serious and I had tried to laugh it off. Could it have been relevant to her accident? Perhaps I should have insisted she tell me there and then instead of making me wait. Would it have made a difference? I could ask André about it when he eventually turned up to pick up her stuff. He might also be able to shed light on the timing of the accident as that also seemed confused. Presumably he would turn up sometime during the day to pick up Sophie's stuff since he hadn't appeared the day before.

Hearing a car out on the lane I stepped out of the door to find out who it was. Lesley and Tim were just about to pull away from their house. I knew they were going to La Rochelle for the day and were intending to stay overnight because they'd said they would be picking up their family from the airport early Monday morning. I saw Lesley utter a few words to Tim before the car slowed to a stop. She then waited patiently for the window to roll down.

"Was that a policeman I saw earlier? Did you tell him about our incident?"

Was she referring to nearly being run off the road or my bag being stolen? Not wanting to spoil Lesley's day I didn't tell her about the suspicions the police had about Sophie's accident, especially because of what had happened to us in her car. She might see connections where there weren't any.

"No...it was about something else...I'll explain later."

She looked disappointed "Oh, ok then. See you later."

"Enjoy your day!" I shouted, looking across Lesley to address both her and Tim.

Tim lifted his hand and waved as he pulled away.

Turning away to go back into the house, I inadvertently walked straight into Mr Saleem. It happened so fast it was difficult to avoid clashing into him. He apologised profusely for not looking where he was going, gesturing toward a newspaper in his hand as if to explain that this had been the focus of his attention.

His look of genuine surprise made me accept his apology warmly.

"It's alright...no harm done."

I stepped back from him, smiling. I'd been as much to blame for not taking any care. I hadn't expected anyone else to be around.

He returned my smile.

"I would like to settle my bill *Madame* but first I have a little favour to ask"

"Oh?" Instinctively I felt a sense of foreboding. He'd clearly sensed my conciliatory attitude and was taking the opportunity to take advantage of the situation.

"Yes...I have the key for *Madame* McCoy's house."

I gave him a quizzical look.

"Yes" he nodded as if to confirm what he said, "she said that I could have a look at the wine in the cellar. They were going to discard it all because of the bottles being submerged in water for so long. They thought it was perhaps ruined. I told them I have a friend who is a collector and he may still be able to sell some of the wine to get some of their money back."

"Right. That sounds great." I nodded, digesting this information. Though not sure what it had to do with me.

"*Madame* McCoy said that if they had gone out to *La Rochelle* before I checked out I could go down to the cellar myself."

And of course they had just left.

"I am then to leave the key with *Monsieur* Sabiron." Seeing my increasingly puzzled look he continued. "Monsieur Sabiron is letting the contractors into the house in the morning to pour the concrete."

I nodded slowly.

"And so... the favour?" still puzzled.

"I wondered if you could show me how to get into the cellar" he paused, an appealing look on his face.

I weighed up his request. On the one hand I knew it wouldn't take too long to do just that but on the other, I was reluctant to spend any more time in his presence if I didn't need to. Unfortunately, my discomfort didn't seem to be a plausible reason to refuse.

"Alright," I agreed. "Shall we go now?"

"If it is convenient? Then I can settle my bill and be on my way."

"Okay."

Despite his current open and friendly look I had experienced his tendency to change manner abruptly and when I least expected it, so it was with some trepidation that I turned and led the way toward Lesley's house. Moments later I stepped aside to allow Mr Saleem to unlock the door and then I swept past him to enter the kitchen. I found the torch lying on one of the counter tops and picked it up, flicking the switch just as I had seen Lesley do only a few days earlier to check it worked. I crossed the kitchen to the cellar door.

Mr Saleem closed the outside door then came up behind me. I grasped the handle and pulled the door open, screwing my face up as the fetid odour hit me.

"It's down there!" I gagged before hastily covering my mouth and nose with my hand. The smell seemed to have gotten worse. The door stayed open itself and I turned on the torch, shining the light down the steps toward the cellar floor then holding it out for Mr Saleem to take. He ignored the offering and peered down into the gloom.

"Could you show me exactly please?" he asked innocently.

I was appalled at the idea but felt reluctant to cause a fuss so despite my better judgement, I grudgingly agreed. Tentatively, I reached for the rail. The quicker I got this over with, the quicker he'd be gone, I thought. Carefully, I picked my way down the steps making the effort to breathe only through my mouth. Mr Saleem followed closely behind. When I reached the cellar floor I lifted the torch and shone the light around the walls before leaving it settled on the wine racks. Wanting to make a swift exit, I held out the torch once again.

"There you are!" My voice was muffled as I'd covered my nose and mouth with my hand, trying to stifle the unpleasant aroma. It was even more putrid than I'd remembered from a few days earlier, perhaps due to the warm weather.

Mr Saleem made no comment so I swung round to look at him, surprised to find that he was showing no sign of being affected by the smell. I also felt rather peeved to see him taking more interest in the tunnel - a tunnel which now had an entrance large enough to walk through after having been investigated further by the *geometre*.

It suddenly struck me that he didn't seem too interested in the wine.

"So the concrete is being poured into the tunnel down here tomorrow" he stated flatly rather than asked.

"Yes..." I replied with rising impatience.

He smiled coldly.

"It is a shame that you had to be dragged into this" he said.

I stared at him, puzzled. Though I tried to persuade myself that he was still discussing the wine, an uneasy feeling took over.

"What...do you mean?"

He moved a step closer to me. Due to the proximity, I could smell his aftershave. A faint musky smell that was still familiar. *Where from?*

Now feeling too close for comfort, I took a step backwards. The wine racks were directly behind me and I felt the wooden edge of the rack dig into my back. Without warning, he grabbed the torch roughly from my hand. I gasped as panic began to rise in me. *What was he doing?*

"Don't pretend you don't know what I'm talking about". He gave me a look of disgust.

"What...do you mean?..." I was completely taken aback, with my thoughts chaotic as I became suddenly aware of my heart pounding in my ears and my mouth going dry. Instinctively checking for an escape route, my gaze flicked toward the cellar steps. Following my look, he stepped sideways to block my path.

"Miss Shakil knew too much. She is a very clever lady. She could put two and two together, but she started making phone calls and sticking her nose in... so..."

Sneering, he leaned in close and slid the wide end of the torch along my jawline. It was cold against my skin. The light shone upwards toward the ceiling. I felt a shiver run down my spine. Felt his breath on my face. I turned my head to the side trying to avoid the proximity.

"She needed to be disposed of" he continued calmly "and now, I have to tidy up loose ends."

I was horrified. *What was he telling me?* That *he* tried to kill Sophie? What loose ends? Did he mean me? What was he going to do with me? I turned my head slightly to look back at him but in the gloom could only just make out the outline of his face.

Intuitively I sensed rather than saw, a gap to the side of him. In a split second I made the decision to make a run for it. *Fight or flight.* He was too big and burly to fight so I had to rely on speed. My speed. With as much haste as I could muster, I darted out to the side and round the back of him toward the steps. Caught unawares he took a moment to respond before swinging round to come after me. The kitchen door at the top of the steps had been left slightly ajar so there was only a very narrow shaft of light for me to use as a guide. In a panic I felt for the rail, hoping to use it to haul myself up the steps more rapidly. Misjudging the distance for my hand to grasp hold, I scrubbed my knuckles hard against the wall. I was oblivious to the pain. All I wanted to do was get away - like an animal trapped in a snare garnering every inch of its being to run for its life.

All of a sudden an agonising pain pierced my scalp. I yelped as my hair was grabbed roughly and used to jerk me backwards.

"Not so fast!" he snapped. I could hear him breathing deeply now and knew now that I had made him angry. Wincing with pain, I cursed myself for not being faster. Still holding onto my hair, he swung me round to look at him. My head twisted and my body arched as I tried to alleviate the throbbing pain he was causing.

"*Please!*" pleading, my voice broke "I don't know about anything...I won't tell anyone what you did" I was rambling, my thoughts unclear. Could I reason with him?

"But don't you have friends in high places?" he smiled at me mockingly, his voice taking on a sinister tone.

I tried to think quickly. *What did he mean?* Frantically I searched my mind for anything he might have heard yet obviously misunderstood. I recalled the conversation with Di about her client. A politician's cousin she'd said. That was the same day Mr Saleem had been leaving the chambres d'hôtes but then changed his mind and backtracked. He must have been listening to our conversation and heard what we'd said. But it wasn't anything to do with him. Surely he couldn't be referring to that? Seeing the look of uncertainty on my face as my thoughts raced, he gave a hollow laugh.

My voice shook, *"But you don't understand...*that was nothing..."

He sighed impatiently and his face took on a menacing look.

"Move into there!" he ordered. Taking his hand from my hair he shoved me forcefully in the middle of my back toward the tunnel entrance. I stumbled and felt my head lightly scrape against a rocky lower part of the ceiling. I winced, stooping as I put my hand against the wall to steady myself. The soil which formed the walls was soft and wet. The torch light flashed ahead and I could see that the ceiling in front of me was even lower so I would need to crouch a little more to move forward. Advancing slowly because of the uneven ground and poor light, I desperately tried to think of how to reason with him, frantically searching my mind. I felt him following closely behind and I began to wonder what he planned to do to with me. I needed to appease him, convince him I wasn't a threat. Unfortunately, time had ran out.

I felt a sudden stab of pain at the back of my head. Everything went black.

CHAPTER TWELVE

I woke up sometime later only semi-conscious in freezing darkness. I could feel the left side of my face and body was slumped heavily against a hard surface. It gradually dawned on me that I was sprawled prostrate on the ground. The side of my face stinging from rough ground digging into it. Using all my effort I brought the palms of my hands onto the earth beneath me. Slowly, pushing against the gravelled dirt, I finally hauled myself into a sitting position. My head ached badly. Intense pain shot through my left knee and I retched with the agony of it. Feeling tentatively around, my fingers cold, wet and virtually numb, I managed to ascertain that there was a wall a few inches to my right side. I lent cautiously towards it and allowed it to support my weight. My head was swimming and I closed my eyes, drifting in an out of consciousness.

After a while I opened my eyes again and managed to keep them open. I felt weary, nauseous. Although too dark to see anything I became aware that I was sitting in about an inch of freezing cold water. Racking my brain frantically to figure out where I was, my thoughts suddenly became clear. I was in the tunnel under Lesley's house. I had shown Mr Saleem down to the cellar. He had become hostile, threatening even. He'd rambled on about me knowing something, or knowing too much. What was it he'd said about Sophie? Something to do with him having her taken care of. I remembered trying to leave but he wouldn't let me. Then he'd pushed me into the tunnel. The back of my head was throbbing. *He must have hit me!* That's why I'm here! I carefully felt for the back of my head at the base of the skull. It was sore to touch and my hair felt matted and sticky. Probably congealed blood I thought grimly.

My God! Realisation dawned. *I had been left for dead!*

Suddenly stricken with panic, I tried to move but pain stabbed through my left knee. I felt dizzy. With both hands I very tentatively felt my way down my thigh toward my knee. I was wearing trousers which were loosely fitted but could feel that the material was now tight around the knee and shin. It must be swollen. I began to give way to feelings of despair. I felt cold, tired, nauseous and in pain. I couldn't see. I couldn't move. Even if I could get up, which way would I go?

Tears pricked my eyes as I let myself get carried away in my wretchedness. I took a few deep breaths. The smell wasn't as bad now; probably just gotten used to it while I'd been there. How long had I been there? I cupped my hands near my mouth and blew into them, trying to warm them. Got to keep it together I told myself. I'm still alive. I can call for help. I listened for noises. What if he was still there? No. Nothing. He was probably long gone. The only noise I could make out sounded like thousands of pebbles dashing against a window. What was that? Aware that I should probably try to get out of the cold water before I got hypothermia, I suddenly realised the water was gradually rising. *Oh no!* The noise I could hear was rain. And during heavy rain the tunnel flooded: that's why Lesley was having it blocked up. *Concrete was going to be poured in.* Grasping the seriousness of my situation, I felt adrenalin course through my body. Of course, he'd left me for dead. It didn't matter that I hadn't been dead when he'd left, I soon would be. Left unconscious to be covered in concrete. Being drowned by the flooding tunnel was probably a bonus. Either way I'd soon be dead.

I had to move. How long had I been there? Could it be nearly morning? It was so dark I couldn't tell. Would they check the tunnel before pouring the concrete? Would they wait till the rain stopped before pumping the water out? It could be really deep by then. Would there be any reason to check the tunnel? They wouldn't expect someone to be in there. I had to get out. How far into the tunnel was I? Which way was out?

I tried to shout but my voice was hoarse from damp and tiredness. I felt dizzy again. Resting my aching head back against the wall I tried to think. A cold breeze hit the right side of my face. Surely there wouldn't be air flowing from the cellar? The cold air must be coming from wherever the tunnel came out. Which meant the way out for me *had* to be the opposite way. *Toward* the cellar. Unless the cellar door was open and that was causing the flow of air. But then surely I would be able to see some glimmer of daylight. Unless it's night time. Lesley and Tim wouldn't be back from La Rochelle till Monday. After the concrete pouring had started. Would they start pouring if it was still raining? If it is still raining the tunnel will flood!

Finding a reserve of strength from somewhere deep inside I made up my mind to move in the opposite direction to the flowing cool air. I hoped and *prayed* it was toward the cellar. I dragged myself along. Bending my right leg to get my heel dug into the ground to give me some leverage, I pushed myself along in a seated position. I didn't have the strength to stand. My hands were numb from the cold water. Just as well I couldn't feel them, knowing how sore they would be from pressing down on the rough ground to lift my weight.

Eventually, I rested against the wall exhausted. My knee and head throbbing. I questioned whether I would be missed. I didn't have any guests. Karl wouldn't be back until late Monday evening. Would anyone notice I was gone?

I imagined I could hear muffled voices. Was I hallucinating now? I opened my mouth to shout for help. Nothing came out. My throat was dry. I gave in to my exhaustion and closed my eyes.

CHAPTER THIRTEEN

Monday

Opening my eyes, I struggled to focus for a few moments. I could still hear rain. But it was a different sound. It was rain against a window pane. And it was light. There was daylight. I swallowed and found my lips were moist. Wriggling fingers and toes which were warm and dry, I went to move.

"Welcome back *Catareen*." I turned my head slowly on the soft pillow toward Marie's warm voice.

"Where..?" I tried to get up.

"No, no. Stay there. Don't be in a 'urry to do anything. The doctor said you must 'ave lots of rest."

I felt some restriction on my arm and looked down to see an intravenous drip had been attached. I frowned.

Marie saw my look.

"You were very de'ydrated when we found you." She explained gently. "The doctor said putting this in was the quickest way to get your body working."

I let my head go heavy against the pillow and looked around at the ceiling and walls, recognising my own bedroom. I felt so happy and relieved to have made it out of that tunnel alive, emotion overwhelmed me and tears slid from my eyes. Marie misinterpreted my tears.

"It's ok now *Catareen*" she said soothingly, "you 'ad an accident and 'it your 'ead but you are going to be ok"

An accident! What about Mr Saleem? I felt too weak to protest.

Marie continued. "We are all a bit unsure of why you were in the tunnel in the first place but you can tell us about that when you are recovered."

My mind whirled.

"The police..." I began.

"The police? Yes. There is an Inspector 'ere. 'e wants to ask you about Mr Saleem. Apparently 'e was not who 'e appeared to be. The Inspector wants to know everything about 'im."

My eyelids felt so heavy as Marie chatted on and on and I struggled to keep my eyes open - drifting off as I heard her say "It can wait."

I slept this time in a deep restful sleep. When I awoke again my vision and thoughts were clearer. Lesley was in the room. She came over to me as soon as she saw me awake.

"Catherine? How are you feeling?...You had a nasty bump on the head there."

"Lesley" I interrupted, attempting to hoist myself up.

Lesley quickly intervened by raising the pillows behind me and helping me to sit more comfortably. The throbbing ache in my head had eased but I winced from the pain in my knee as she helped me to move.

"You must get the police. I need to speak to someone about Mr Saleem."

"Mr Saleem?" she said in surprise "yes, of course."

Lesley busied herself putting the duvet straight without any sense of urgency. She continued.

"A police Inspector has been hanging around waiting to speak to you about him. I must say I'm surprised they think anything odd about him. I found him quite charming..."

"Lesley, *please*..." I said in an exasperated tone.

Seeing her hurt look, I instantly regretted my manner.

Her voice faltered "I'll ...go and fetch him."

She hurried out of the room only to return moments later with a thin rangy man with hard features. She introduced him as Inspector Maupetit. He was a plain clothes policeman of medium height who wore drab, grey trousers. A light jacket covered a thin cream coloured shirt. His balding head looked shaven rather than from a natural loss of hair and I wondered whether he thought it gave him a tough look to make made up for his petite stature.

Despite his rather hangdog expression, Inspector Maupetit's manner was polite and friendly.

"*Bonjour Madame* Patterson". He looked at me with interest "I am sorry to 'ear about your accident. If you are strong enough, I need to ask you some questions." He paused, thinking. "We are trying to piece together what 'as been 'appening 'ere."

Lesley interrupted. Looking at me matter of factly she said, "I'll be downstairs if you need me."

Feeling guilty at my harshness earlier I gave her an exaggerated look of gratitude.

"Thank you so much Lesley."

She beamed. I was back in her good books.

The inspector waited for Lesley to leave then turned back to me.

"First of all, *Madame*, 'ow did you find Monsieur Saleem?" He walked over to the chair in the corner of the room and perched himself on the end of it.

"Inspector, this" I waved a hand at my bedridden posture "was not an accident."

He remained silent. His eyes alert.

I continued "*Monsieur* Saleem *attacked* me. He lured me into the cellar on the pretence of looking at wine. Then he turned on me. Accused me of knowing too much or of knowing about something. I couldn't make head nor tail of it."

"'ead nor tail?" the Inspector looked at me in confusion.

"Sorry. I mean I couldn't understand what he was talking about. He became very hostile and pushed me into the tunnel." The memory of it made me shiver. I continued.

"He knew about the concrete being poured and left me for dead!" My voice became shrill. Anxiety overwhelming me at the thought of what had happened. I fought to remain calm.

The Inspector digested this information but took it in his stride.

"Yes, *Madame*. I think per'aps you were saved by the rain. They could not pour the concrete because of it. And your friends of course, Marie and *Madame* McCoy, came to your rescue when they realised you were missing."

I was struck by his use of Marie's first name, wondering if they were known to each other while considering his words.

So the rain had stopped them pouring the concrete and I had also been missed – thank goodness for Marie and Lesley!

"I 'ave spoken to *Mademoiselle* Shakil about *Monsieur* Saleem."

Sophie! I had almost forgotten about poor Sophie. The Inspector continued.

"She tells me that *Monsieur* Saleem told you 'e was Egyptian. But *Mademoiselle* Shakil was suspicious when 'e didn't act in such a way that would betray 'im as an Egyptian."

"Huh?" I didn't know what he meant.

"You know...er...the manners, characteristic...things which are particular to different nationalities."

"I see..." What was he saying? If a Frenchman was pretending to be an Englishman he would be betrayed by the smell of garlic and a trail of empty snail shells? Surely it couldn't be that simple. Yet Sophie must have somehow suspected he wasn't what he seemed. She must have tried to check him out. She'd said she had a few phone calls to make. Was that what she had tried to tell me before she went out that evening? Lowering her voice in such a way that Mr Saleem couldn't hear her and then purposely ignoring him on the way to her car?

"*Mademoiselle* Shakil also tells me that she 'as worked before as an investigative journalist. She knows 'ow to investigate." He nodded knowingly. It was something she had mentioned but not to any great detail. But then I hadn't known her long.

"But, surely Inspector you're not telling me these incidents were just because Mr Saleem wasn't Egyptian? It makes no sense!"

"Ah *Madame.* There is a bigger picture. The brakes on *Mademoiselle's* car were definitely cut. We know that for sure. When my officer came 'ere to speak to you, he 'ad the foresight to write down the registration number of the other car parked 'ere which is of course now gone." He looked down at the notes in his hand "it was an 'ire car, which was rented by a *Monsieur* Saleem. 'owever" he looked at me directly " 'is papers did not check out. They were false. We 'ave therefore checked CCTV where 'e 'ired the car and 'ave a picture of 'is face. This 'as been run through our computers and we now 'ave 'is name as *Ibrahim Hussein*, a Libyan wanted in connection with certain irregular activities in Libya."

"And what has that to do with us?" Still baffled.

He sighed. "At the moment *Madame* we are not sure. We do not know why 'e was 'ere. We do not know what 'e 'ad on 'is agenda. We only know that *Mademoiselle* Shakil blew 'is cover and 'e believed you to know about 'im too. 'E needed to dispose of you both before you contacted the authorities."

He gave a Gallic shrug.

"What better way? *Mademoiselle* Shakil in a car accident? And you completely disappearing under concrete?...It was only because of the vigilance of my sergeant who visited you yesterday that we were able to find out who Mr Saleem was."

I nodded, remembering the *gendarme* taking a close look at the cars before leaving. A thought struck me but I hesitated, thinking it was of no relevance.

"My friend's husband works in Libya."

The Inspector regarded me intently, waiting for me to continue.

"He was recently questioned about someone's death. The person he was questioned about supposedly died in suspicious circumstances. They...the police...believed him to be the last person to see her alive."

The Inspector gave me his full attention. " 'Er?"

"She was his interpreter." I paused "Do you think it could be connected?"

The Inspector suddenly reached into the inside pocket of his jacket. He pulled out his phone and studied it for a few seconds.

"Excuse me *Madame*. I must take this."

He got up from the chair and went outside. Out of earshot. Minutes later he returned, a thoughtful look on his face.

"*Madame*... 'as your friend's 'usband given you anything recently?"

"Given *me* anything?" I shook my head.

" 'e 'as not brought anything back for you from Libya, perhaps as a gift?" he persisted.

"Not for me. No... For Di...Yes...A scarf?" I shrugged. How can this be important? The Inspector was silent. I attempted to clarify.

"A silk scarf, embroidered, sequined...very beautiful."

"I see" he moved toward the window looking out onto the garden. He remained silent for a few minutes longer then turned toward me.

"I must confess I do not know why you 'ave become of such interest to your guest"

"*Interest?*"

Once again he paused for several moments before sighing heavily.

"*Madame*, the man you know as Mr Saleem is a known assassin."

"*What?*" Shock and fear.

"I did not want to frighten you but I am struggling to figure out 'ow you were a target for 'im."

He shook his head then continued "Per'aps I will find out more when I 'ave made more enquiries."

He turned to go then stopped himself

"This is a guest 'ouse *madame?*"

I nodded

"Do you 'ave any other guests?"

"No, not at the moment, apparently my website was sabotaged."

Suddenly it dawned on me that it was perhaps Mr Saleem who'd sabotaged it. The Inspector saw my look of realisation.

"Yes," he nodded in agreement, guessing my thoughts " 'e probably wanted you alone."

A thought occurred.

"Di, my friend, thought she had had an intruder a few nights ago. Do you think it could be connected?"

"Per 'aps" his tone was non-committal.

"*And*...I was followed from her house by a maniac driver..." My thoughts were flooding back with an increasing feeling of anxiety "...the driver was also at the village fête. I saw him watching me ...but it wasn't

Mr Saleem...it was another man...who oddly enough looked similar in stature and colouring."

"Mmm... these people can sometimes work in cells" he nodded matter of factly, acknowledging my words yet still seeming unsure about how to piece the information together.   Then suddenly, as if deciding on a course of action, he made to leave.

"I will no doubt return to let you know about my enquiries Madame."

He took a small business card out of his front jacket pocket. "If you think of anything else, my number is 'ere."

He put the card down next to the phone on the dresser.

"Thank you for your 'elp."

After the Inspector had left I went over things in my mind. Was there anything that had happened which I was missing but would help to make sense of all this?

I tried to link up the chain of events. Mr Saleem turned up on Friday evening. I hadn't been able to open the door from the hallway into the house. The key wouldn't work. I thought it was because I'd had too much to drink but the following day the key still didn't work. Yet Mr Saleem, or whatever his name was, opened it straightaway. No, surely I'm overthinking this. A problem with a lock doesn't mean anything. Unless...I surveyed the room. The morning after his arrival I had a lot of tidying up to do in the bedroom because it was in such a mess. I'd blamed myself because I thought I'd messed it up in my inebriated state after returning from the fête. But why would I go rummaging through drawers before going to sleep? What if? No! What if...the room had been *searched*? Wouldn't it have looked like that? A few clothes left hanging out. A few ornaments moved out of place which were only noticeable to the person living there. Did Mr Saleem try to pick the lock to get into the house? Is that why it doesn't work now? Did I come home too early? Perhaps he couldn't get into the house and was forced to pretend to be a paying guest. Then, when I was asleep, both outer and hallway door unlocked, he came to search my bedroom while knowing I was out for the count because I'd overindulged with alcohol. *My God!* He could've murdered me there and then! Why didn't he? Because...what did the Inspector say?. ..he might be looking for something? And because he didn't find what he was looking for, he stayed as a paying guest for longer? Realisation dawned. Is that why his aftershave was familiar? Because he'd been in my bedroom? Aghast, I lay back on the pillows feeling very perturbed yet at the same time marvelling at how lucky I'd been. An *assassin*! Wait till Karl hears about this! I lay for some time continuing to mull over the events of the past few days. What about the other guy at the fête watching me? Was he the look out? Waiting to see how long I'd be there while Mr Saleem searched the house? And why had he acted menacingly anyway? Surely, the idea according to the Inspector was that they only attacked me and Sophie because we were getting too close? But what were they looking for?

I sighed heavily. This was all guesswork. I still didn't have a clue. My head was starting to ache. I reached over to take a couple of pain killers left by the doctor and washed them down with the water Lesley had left by the bedside.

I lay there dozing for a while before Marie arrived.

"Changing shift!" she announced breezily as she approached the bed. Lesley appeared from behind.

"I'll leave you in good hands" Lesley said cheerfully.

"Lesley, wait!" I struggled to sit up again. Both of them moved quickly to help me.

"I wanted to thank you both. The Inspector told me that it was you two who found me. You saved my life."

They exchanged blank looks then Marie spoke.

"If it wasn't for *Monsieur* Ferret we might not 'ave found you."

"*Monsieur Ferret?*"

"*Oui*" said Marie. Lesley nodded supportively.

"*Monsieur* Ferret was tending his vegetables yesterday morning in 'is garden, as 'e usually does and saw you going into Lesley's 'ouse with Mr Saleem. 'e noticed Mr Saleem leave in 'is car later but did not see you go back to your 'ouse. When you did not appear at the van this morning 'e mentioned that 'e 'ad not seen you since yesterday morning although your car was still there. I, of course, was not expecting you at the van because I knew you did not 'ave guests 'ere today. I assumed *Monsieur* Ferret just 'ad a suspicious nature. But then on my round I bumped into André. 'e asked if I knew if you would be 'ere this morning because when 'e came yesterday afternoon to pick up Sophie's belongings, 'e couldn't find you. I began to feel that something was not right."

She paused and Lesley took over.

"You remember we were picking our family up from *La Rochelle* airport? Well, we arrived back here this morning around nine thirty. Marie was talking to *Monsieur* Sabiron. I had told Mr Saleem he could leave the key with *Monsieur* Sabiron so that the contractors could get on with the job of pouring concrete as soon as they arrived. Of course it was raining heavily. By the time we got here, the contractors had already left. They told *Monsieur* Sabiron that they had checked the cellar but it was flooding too quickly. They would have to return on a dry day and after the water had been pumped out again."

I shook my head slowly in disbelief. All of that time I'd been in the tunnel. Most of Sunday *and* through the night.

"So how did you know where I was?"

Marie took over again.

"*Monsieur* Ferret said that 'e 'adn't seen you come out of Lesley's 'ouse. I told Lesley that we couldn't find you..." she looked toward Lesley for confirmation. "...we thought it unlikely but we decided to go down to the cellar to check." She paused thinking. "It was by then knee deep in water and very cold.

"Freezing" agreed Lesley, nodding.

"We saw you near the entrance to the tunnel. Propped up against the wall." She paused, blinking back tears. "We thought you were dead."

They both fell silent, allowing us all time to digest the information. I couldn't believe how lucky I had been. I also made a mental note to try harder in my efforts to communicate with *Monsieur* Ferret.

Consumed with emotion they both came toward me and the three of us embraced each other warmly. It felt so heartening to have such good friends.

I pulled back from them.

"I just can't thank you enough." My voice was thick with emotion.

Marie spoke first

"Well now it is all over and you must concentrate on being well."

"Yes. And I will see you later. Take care." Lesley kissed me on the cheek and left.

"Karl will be home around nine. He can take over then." I suggested.

"It is no bother to stay" replied Marie "The rain 'as stopped and the air 'as cooled a little. It is turning into a pleasant evening. I will enjoy the walk home."

At that point the doctor arrived. It was so late in the afternoon, I'd assumed I wouldn't see him till the following day. Hearing our voices, he'd let himself in and came straight up to the bedroom. As a courtesy, he knocked on the bedroom door.

"*Pierre!*"

Marie greeted him warmly like an old friend, kissing on both cheeks. The young, thirtysomething doctor had thick dark hair and was of medium height. He wore round, Harry Potter like spectacles and was carrying his bag of tricks.

He approached the bed.

"*Bonjour Madame.* 'ow are you feeling?"

Without waiting for a reply, he took his attention to the drip bag and then removed the tube from my arm before beginning to dismantle the stand.

"A lot better. Thank you."

He took hold of my wrist and studied his watch to check my pulse then he placed his bag on the foot of the bed and rummaged through it before producing a thermometer. Shaking it as he leaned in toward me, I opened my mouth obediently.

"Do you feel 'ungry?" I nodded a reply, conscious of not wanting to disturb the thermometer still in my mouth.

"Good. You are recovering well *Madame*. I am glad we did not need to take you off to the 'ospital".

Moments later he took the thermometer from my mouth and studied it for a few seconds before putting it away. Sitting on the edge of the bed, he scrutinised me closely.

"Your 'ead will 'urt for a few days but the pain will wear off. And your leg. 'ow does it feel?"

"Aching."

"The knee 'as a lot of bruising but no permanent damage. It will recover with rest." He paused "You are very lucky to be alive *Madame*."

I made no comment, touched by everyone's concern and care.

The doctor stood up and breathed a huge sigh.

"I must go now." He said briskly. "You should 'ave enough pain killers for the next few days. If you need more, per'aps your 'usband can call by my surgery?"

"Of course. Thank you."

Marie showed the doctor out and then several minutes later delivered a small bowl of light onion *consommé*. It was delicious and she admitted that it was one of her husband's specialities. She told me he liked to cook and thought of himself as something of a gourmet despite his faults. It occurred to me that a lot of the French had the same opinion of themselves. Marie sat chatting happily by my bedside and I was glad of her company but felt sleepy after eating and began to doze. Sensing my fatigue she quietened but remained seated next to the bed.

Unfortunately sleep did not come easily as my mind remained active in attempts to piece together recent events. Mr Saleem or Mr Hussein, as he was also known was Libyan. He'd searched my room looking for something. The only thing I knew that had been brought back from Libya was the scarf. Could it be the scarf he was looking for? The scarf I had had it in my possession for most of this last week. It had been in my bag in the car. But how would he know I had it? I picked it up in the café. Could the man I saw smoking in the car park, the one I'd suspected of following me out have been part of this? Could he have alerted Mr Saleem to me having the scarf? While I was at the fête did he try to get into the house to search for it? Then not being able to find it perhaps he'd entered my bedroom while I was asleep to look for it? Still unable to find it, he'd acted like any usual guest, maybe hoping to come across it while he was here?

The trip to the caves with Lesley crossed my mind. Did someone follow us there? Maybe it wasn't my imagination that someone was lurking in the shadows and watching us in the underground church. Did that same person take my bag in the café to search it? And the silver car? Was it that same person coming from the hamlet after a *rendez vous* with Mr Saleem that nearly ran us off the road?

I sighed. So many unanswered questions. What was it all about? I thought back to Mr Saleem's appearance when I'd returned the scarf to Di on Saturday. How odd it seemed when he'd returned to the chambres d'hôtes only moments after leaving! He must have seen the scarf then and overheard us talk about a politician's cousin! If indeed it is the scarf that he's after. Maybe he then thought we were going to pass it on to someone else? Is that why he was trying to kill me? Because he thought we knew something about the scarf and were about to pass it on to someone connected to someone more powerful? *What was it about the scarf?* It had been given to Phil by his interpreter. This interpreter had purportedly committed suicide. Surely that's the connection with Libya. *But why was the scarf so important?* I tried to remember whether I'd told the Inspector that it was the interpreter that had given Phil the scarf. The interpreter whose death Phil had originally been arrested for. Maybe the Inspector could have made sense of it, though he didn't seem to know much, I thought wryly. Racking my brain for anything else that could be relevant, I continued trying to piece it all together.

It occurred to me that Di now had the scarf. She had also had an intruder. Was the intruder part of this? Were they after the scarf? Why on earth did they want it? Mr Saleem had tried to dispose of both Sophie and me. What if Di was next? She could at this very moment be in danger.

CHAPTER FOURTEEN

Making a split decision to get out of bed, I swung my feet down to touch the floor and instantly felt dizzy. Karl was there. I hadn't even noticed he'd arrived and Marie had left. He came over immediately.

"Woah easy!" He shooed me back into bed.

"Karl!" we embraced warmly. It was good to see his familiar face.

"So I've been brought up to date." He looked at me bemused. "Marie told me Inspector..." he stopped to think " er... *Clouseau*'s been here."

I smiled at his attempt at humour.

He shook his head in disbelief.

"It seems I leave you alone for a few days and you get yourself involved in some sort of international espionage." He grimaced. "I shouldn't jest. You're lucky to be alive by all accounts."

I ignored his comments. There were other things more pressing.

"Karl, I think Di's in danger. I think it's the scarf they're after...Can you phone Di? I need to check she's ok."

"*What?*" He looked mystified but seeing my earnest look, he allowed himself to be coerced "Sure. No problem." Shaking his head in bafflement, he went to the dresser and picked up the phone. He knew Di's number was on speed dial so he didn't need to ask for it. After holding the phone to his ear for a good few minutes he shook his head.

"It's just ringing."

"*Oh God!*" I began to feel dread, my stomach clenching in fear.

"Now...just a minute." He said firmly and calmly. "Don't panic yet. D'you have her mobile phone number?"

"Yes it's on mine- in my bag." I pointed to the bag left discarded on the floor next the chair in the corner. Karl rummaged through it and pulled out my mobile phone.

He studied it for a moment.

"There's not much charge left on it. I'll try it anyway."

He took a few moments to find the number then put it to his ear. I felt tense, willing Di to answer her phone.

Again he shook his head.

"Just going to answer phone."

My voice was pleading. "We've *got* to get in touch with the Inspector. His card is there on the dresser next to the phone."

Karl went to pick it up then hesitated, looking at me thoughtfully.

"I could just phone the police instead and say I think a friend is in trouble. They might do a sort of drive by to check."

"*No.*" I shook my head, anxiously. "It's a waste of time! They've been out once this week. They thought Di was crazy. In fact, they might not even bother going to the house."

He looked back at the card and with an air of resignation.

"Ok. I'll phone the Inspector."

A few moments later he shook his head again.

"Answer phone."

I was becoming increasingly fearful. Di was alone. She might well have a gun but she was certainly not a match for trained killers.

"Karl we have to go to Di's. Check she's ok."

"*We?* You can't go anywhere!"

"*Please* Karl" I implored him "I'll stay in the car. I promise. I can try to get hold of the Inspector while you drive."

He deliberated for a moment, torn between allowing me to interrupt my convalescence and rushing toward a potentially life threatening situation to help a friend.

He gave an exasperated sigh.

"Alright...but you must stay in the car. I'll go into the house to check on Di."

"Fine." I pulled back the covers.

"You'll have to help me to the car" I said sheepishly.

He looked at my leg anxiously and I could see he was having second thoughts.

Reluctantly he agreed.

"Right" his voice tense.

He helped me to pull on sweatpants and shirt and I had the foresight to pick up a couple of pain killers to numb the expected pain in my leg from standing.

With Karl supporting my weight I hobbled alongside him to get to the car. Feeling light headed as I climbed awkwardly into the passenger seat, I refused to admit how weak I felt. I was determined to help Di. Karl watched me keenly as I put on my seat belt but he said nothing. He passed me his mobile phone and the Inspector's card.

"Keep trying" He paused. "I'd rather he got there first rather than us, even if ..." he didn't finish.

"Right." Even if we can help Di or even if *we're too late?*

Karl pulled the car out onto the main road. The roads to Di's house were pitch black. There were no street lights and for most of the way Karl used full beam, driving more cautiously than usual. I knew Karl hated driving in the dark and felt guilty that I was putting him through this, especially if I was wrong and Di was ok. My mind was still racing. What significance was the scarf? What was so special about it? All we knew was that it was given to Phil by someone who was now dead.

I stared into the darkness. What a fool I'd been not to have seen through Mr Saleem. I should have trusted my gut instinct when I felt uneasy and done something about it then instead of telling myself each time that I was mistaken. But what could I have done? A trained killer stays as my guest and I think that I can do, what, confront him? Is that what Sophie did? Had she made it obvious she was onto him? Did that account for the time difference between leaving André's house and crashing her car? Mr Saleem had gone out late that night. Could it have been to meet Sophie? Maybe she had agreed to a meeting related to his pretence. But why? For information? Didn't the Inspector say she used to be an investigative reporter? So had she put herself in danger? And Mr Saleem or Hussein or whatever his name was or his accomplice had been able to use the opportunity to cut the brake cable in her car. To shut her up? To protect himself?

I suddenly lurched forward in my seat as the car came to an abrupt halt. A large stag stood on the road ahead looking magnificent in the beam of the headlights. I couldn't help but marvel at the majesty of the creature before us while also desperately willing it to move. Without any sense of urgency it remained stock still, appearing as if it was deliberately taking its time to weigh up whether we were a threat or not. Then, as if concluding we were of no further interest, it strolled casually across to the other side of the road.

Though in a hurry to reach Di's house, Karl pulled the car away as smoothly and quietly as he could rather than startle the animal further while I made additional attempts to contact the Inspector. It was to no avail. Both Di's and the Inspector's mobile phone just kept going to messages.

At long last, we pulled into the lane which led up to Di's house. I felt like my eyes were out on stalks as I leaned forward, trying to peer into the blackness for any sign of an intruder.

Just then we heard a loud bang. Karl quickly pulled the car over to the side of the road before the turning for Di's house. He turned off the engine. We looked at each other in alarm. Was it a gunshot?

I voiced our thoughts with a whisper.

"Did that sound like a gun?"

Karl grimaced and shrugged.

"Could've been." He paused. "We should really call the local police. It's not like we can protect ourselves if that was a gunshot...And what if it's Di firing?...She might not realise it's us...Try her phone again."

He switched on the inside light above the rear view mirror so I could see what I was doing, watching while I pressed a couple of buttons for redial. At that moment, the door on the driver's side was flung open. We both gasped and recoiled in fright as a burly man wearing dark clothes and a black woollen balaclava leaned in towards us. He swiftly pulled up the balaclava to reveal a solemn, rugged face.

"Turn off that light" he hissed, speaking in English with a french accent. I obeyed immediately, fumbling for the switch.

"*Monsieur et Madame* Patterson?" His voice little more than a whisper.

We both nodded, terrified. "Yes," replied Karl.

"You must not go any further. Your friend is in danger but we 'ave everything under control."

Both Karl and I were visibly relieved.

"We? Who..?" I began.

He didn't let me finish.

"The *politician's cousin Madame*." A grin flicked across his face as he saw my look of recognition mixed with confusion.

"I'll explain later. For now," he looked at both of us keenly. "You must stay 'ere. *Do not* leave until one of my men tell you it is okay."

We both nodded readily confirming our willingness to do so. He then closed the door carefully and quietly and left us in the dark.

Karl lowered his voice, looking at me in amazement.

"What's he on about? The *politician's cousin*?"

I could sense his frustration at being left out of the loop. I could also understand how he felt. He'd returned from England and found all hell had broken loose in his normal comfortable surroundings and he still didn't quite have a clue about what was going on. I began to explain in a whisper about Di and the exhibition room. How she'd met someone who was supposed to be the cousin of some prominent politician. Just then another shot rang out. We both flinched in our seats.

My voice was little more than a murmur.

"*Oh God!* Wish we knew what was going on. D'you think we're safe here?"

Before Karl had time to answer, a bright flash light shone toward the windscreen of the car. We both shielded our eyes against the glare. There were people shouting outside. Someone, who I could only make out from the chest down due to the brightness of the light, strode purposefully toward us. He was dressed all in black and was carrying a handgun. I braced myself, hoping desperately that he wasn't hostile. He came to my side of the car and roughly pulled the door open.

"*Messieur Dames.* Okay?" he said gruffly holstering his gun.

We nodded, still unsure whether he was friend or foe.

"Okay?" he repeated loudly then gestured for us to get out of the car. Despite his brusque manner his face was friendly and I suspected his lack of conversation was due to his lack of English.

I ventured a query.

"*Madame Harley est ok? Nous pouvons aller chez elle maintenant?*"

I asked if we could go to her house. He looked relieved that he did not have to converse in English.

"*Oui, madame. D'accord. Vous pouvez y aller.*"

Looking surprised, he moved back a step as Karl started up the engine, probably assuming that we would get out to walk the last few metres to the house. I knew Karl was thinking of my injury, so headlights switched on, Karl moved the car slowly the short distance to the parking area in front of Di's house.

The whole house was lit up. As Karl came round to my side of the car to help me out, four hefty men, all dressed in the same regular black outfits, faces still covered, crossed our path. Though none of them glanced in our direction, I doubted they were oblivious to our presence. Their boots crunched heavily on the gravel path as they carried between them a long black, weighty looking, polythene type bag –just about the size for a body. We watched, horrified, as they heaved it unceremoniously into the back of a large black SUV. One of them slammed the back door shut and in turn they all leapt into the car. It pulled away at some speed. We stood still, transfixed, and watched it disappear from sight.

Finally turning toward the house I noticed there was still one other car parked next to Di's which was still unaccounted for. Karl offered me his support and looked at me in bemusement.

"Well! Let's go and see what's been going on."

I held onto him as I hobbled into the house. Di sat at the kitchen table with Jess lying at her feet. She flounced her tail against the tiled floor but made no effort to rise in greeting. Opposite Di sat the man who several minutes earlier had pulled open our car door and ordered us to stay put. He had removed his balaclava and the brightness of the kitchen showed up every line in his rugged features. Di looked up as we entered, her strained look changing to one of horror on seeing me struggling into the room. The man went to pull over a chair. Karl got to it first which was just as well since it was at that moment that I started to feel faint with the effort of walking.

Seeming depleted of energy, Di remained seated. Her shoulders sagged.

"Oh Catherine I'm so sorry" she put her head in her hands for a moment then looked up at me, her eyes wet. "It's my fault for getting you into this. If I hadn't left that damn scarf..."

I looked from her to the man in confusion. There were still gaps in my knowledge. Karl spoke up.

"Can somebody *please* tell me what's going on?"

The man looked at Di as if checking she could cope. She nodded at him.

He launched into the explanation, his voice authoritative and his wording precise.

"*Monsieur* Patterson" he looked at Karl for a moment then directed his gaze at me. "*Madame.*" He paused a moment as if collecting his thoughts.

"'ow much do you know of the background to the civilian struggle against Colonel Gaddafi in Libya?"

Karl and I looked at each other, puzzled, then back to the man.

"Just what was said on the news when it happened...in the papers." Karl said.

The man nodded "Of course. Most people know only what is reported." He paused again and I assumed he was struggling with how much information he could give us. Then, he sighed resignedly, as if realising we were entitled to a full explanation.

"It is not important that you know my name. It is enough for you to know that I work for French intelligence."

He paused a moment to let us digest this information. I glanced at Karl who was sitting open-mouthed in astonishment. I was too tired and uncomfortable to be amazed.

"A while ago we 'ad information that one of the insurgents who had 'elped to topple Gaddafi 'ad knowledge of a particular group of men who were plotting to disrupt the interim government. These men had been Amazigh fighters who believed that if it wasn't for the Amazigh forces, the tide would never 'ave turned in favour of the revolutionaries at that time."

Sensing, rather than seeing our confusion he continued as if explaining to a child.

"The Amazigh are Libyan people who were marginalised under Gadaffi. It is common knowledge that they 'ad expected this to continue even with a new government. The men I speak of are in a position to disrupt the national transitional council. The insurgent who gave this information about the planned disruption 'ad unwittingly become closely linked with this group of men. 'e came to us because he knew of this plot and 'oped the west could influence the new government; getting them to allow the Amazigh identity to be included in Libya's new constitution and for Tamazight to be made an official language alongside Arabic. If they did this there would be no need for disruption and Libya would remain in this peaceful transition...You see this insurgent I speak of believed the disruption in the name of their cause would not strengthen it but do the opposite. It would make the Amizigh people persecuted even more. The Amazigh would still be bitter and turn their bitterness into a new armed struggle... Unfortunately the men found out that this insurgent 'ad betrayed them and killed him...Suspecting 'is life was in danger, 'e stored the information which included the names of these men and their plans on a micro SD card."

Karl rubbed a hand over his eyes and showed his exasperation by exhaling loudly through puffed cheeks. He looked at the man in disbelief.

"That is a *lot* to take in..." He began "...but let's get this straight...all this has to do with a guy in Libya who had information about a group he was a part of...but didn't like their way of doing things...so he stole information then got himself killed by the very people he was allied with?"

The man nodded, waiting for it all to sink in.

Trying to make sense of his words, I thought back to the events over the last few days and the penny slowly began to drop.

"So Saleem and his men were after the information?"

"That's right *Madame*. The insurgent who was killed gave it to his sister. A woman known to Mr 'arley as *Ayesha Ahmed*. She managed to insert it securely into the narrow 'em of the scarf...because of the sequins, it was not apparent."

Di looked aghast "The interpreter!"

He nodded and went on "Her brother *Yousef*, told 'er that if anything 'appened to 'im she must pass it on to the 'Frenchman'. Unfortunately, we think that 'e didn't 'ave the chance to tell 'er 'ow to get to the 'Frenchman', his contact, before 'e was killed. The men found out 'e 'ad seen 'is sister and suspected she must 'ave the information. Knowing 'er brother 'ad been murdered she decided to leave, knowing that she too was in danger. She gave the scarf to Monsieur 'arley, we suspect... because she didn't know who else to pass it to, needed to keep it safe and ...it was the only Frenchman she knew."

"And...they murdered her?" whispered Di.

Karl looked confused "But Phil's not..." he began.

"*Non Monsieur*, 'e is not French. 'e is an Englishman working for an American company. There are many English working there. We think *Monsieur* 'arley was the only one she 'ad any contact with who she knew lived in France. She was desperate to get rid of it so...we *think* ...but do not know...that she 'oped *Monsieur* 'arley was the right Frenchman...We also think that they killed 'er before she 'ad a chance to find out."

He paused as if expecting further interruptions. Satisfied that we had nothing to add, he continued.

"We think *Ayesha Ahmed* fabricated a story about 'aving to leave and go back 'ome so she could give *Monsieur* 'arley the scarf. We think that during 'er captivity she was questioned about what she 'ad done with the information. They suspected she 'ad passed it on but we think...they did not know *'ow*" He shrugged and paused for a moment. "Then they killed 'er...freeing her hands to make it look initially like a suicide."

Karl interrupted "So they knew she'd given the information to Phil but not where it was hidden?"

"That is correct. 'er brother was in contact with us, the French intelligence, but we think that 'e was killed before 'e could tell his sister who 'is contact was."

"And what was the supposed cause of her suicide? That she couldn't live without her brother?..."

Again the man shrugged. "She 'ad also lost her parents. They were killed in an air strike on Benghazi by Gaddafi's forces before the no fly zone was put into effect by the west."

"Dear God!"

"Knowing that *Ayesha* had been in contact before 'er capture with *Monsieur* 'arley, they dispatched people, the man you know as Saleem, and 'is men, to France to take back the information. Even though, we *suspect*, they were still not sure where the information was."

Again he paused, allowing us time to digest what he had said. He seemed to *suspect* a lot, rather than know it for fact. I thought back to the café and the conversation about where Di's scarf had come from. Could we have been overheard discussing the interpreter? That could be how they'd found out the information was on the scarf. Racking my brain I thought back to that day and groaned aloud as it dawned on me that I'd been sure someone was following me out to the car park. Though I'd thought initially that I was imagining it, I had then seen a man smoking a cigarette as I'd left the car park. Could it have been him?

The man was watching me intently.

"I think there was someone in the restaurant who was listening to us talking...They must have heard Di say that Phil had brought the scarf back from Libya...Obviously, we gave them the exact information they were looking for...I also had the feeling that I was followed out of the restaurant."

I remembered the family I had moved out of the way to avoid. Wondering now if I should silently thank them for being around so that the cigarette man was unable to make his move.

The man nodded.

"That would explain it...'ow they knew the scarf contained the SD card 'as been a mystery to us..." He paused, thinking.

"When the local police questioned *Monsieur* 'arley about 'is connection to the interpreter, 'e came to our attention. We did not know at first why 'e was part of this. Then our agents in France became aware that *Madame* 'arley was being followed...Of course, when you, *Madame* Patterson picked up the scarf, you were also brought into this er...situation. They despatched the man you know as *Monsieur* Saleem to get the scarf from you. When 'e was unable to find it and *Mademoiselle* Shakil questioned 'im about 'is origins. Yes *Madame*," seeing my look of dismay. "She suspected 'e was not the Egyptian 'e claimed to be...'e decided to not leave any loose ends. 'e attempted to kill *Madamoiselle* Shakil. Then 'e decided you too 'ad to die. 'e did not know whether *Mademoiselle* Shakil 'ad told you of her suspicions which you could then tell to the authorities. But also *Madame*, this *Monsieur* Saleem saw you pass the scarf back to *Madame* 'arley. Believing *Madame* 'arley to be part of this, 'e, I think, could not be sure that you were not in ca'oots with someone to whom you could pass on the information. And also, once 'e knew where the scarf was, you were of no further use to 'im."

"D'you mean he thought we *knew* about the information on the SD card?" As I said this I realised it to be true. In Lesley's cellar, *Monsieur* Saleem had accused me of passing information on to someone. Wasn't it the *'politician's cousin'* he'd said? Because he'd heard us talk about this.

"I think *Monsieur* Saleem believed Di and I knew about the information hidden on the scarf because I think he overheard us talk about her knowing a *'politician's* cousin' at the same time I was handing the scarf back to her"

"What is this about a *politician's cousin?*" interrupted Karl.

The man sighed. "When I first approached *Madame* 'arley about a painting..."

Astonished at the revelation that this was the same man who'd wanted to commission a painting, I looked at Di for confirmation. She sat, utterly exhausted, staring ahead vacantly.

"You must understand *Messieurs Dames* that I 'ad to use my pretence to speak to *Madame* 'arley, to gain 'er confidence. We needed to be sure she was unaware that the scarf had sensitive information 'eld on it. We 'ad to get rid of our suspicion that *Monsieur* 'arley might know about the information and was not, in fact, in league with the plotters. Of course, we quickly discovered, as we suspected, that none of you were involved in any of this. You were merely innocent bystanders and *Monsieur* 'arley used only to get rid of the information."

Searching our faces momentarily to check we were following, the man continued "...I told Madame 'arley about being a 'politician's cousin' because I wanted her to have a sort of code word"

"*A what?*"

The man began to look impatient at Karl's interruptions.

"If...as I suspected...Madame 'arley was not involved, then I believed 'er to be in great danger. I...could not tell 'er this because..." The man began to look uncomfortable. "...we needed 'er to act normally...to draw the assassin out into the open"

I stared at him open mouthed. Did he mean *she was bait?*

"If she got into difficulty and we 'ad to 'elp 'er, then I or one of my men would be able to 'elp...they could mention the *'politician's cousin'*. I knew she would believe them to be genuine because of this."

Just as I had done, when someone unknown to me, had opened the car door sometime earlier in the evening. I nodded in understanding, astounded by how much they knew about our movements and conversations. All of those times I had told myself I was being paranoid. The person who had followed me out of the café while the scarf was in my bag, the insane driver who turned up at the fête, the feeling that someone had been behind us in the underground church as well as disbelief that my bag had being taken. Not to mention, the fact that our house had been *searched.* And the man I knew as Mr Saleem had completely fooled me. I felt a complete idiot. As if sensing my thoughts, the man looked at me directly and said soothingly.

"These were professionals *Madame.* Used to accomplishing their mission then disappearing without trace. Luckily for us, this time they were sloppy. We now 'ave two of them out of the picture and an end to their mission."

"How so?"

"They know we now 'ave the SD card so will not take any further action 'ere. We 'ave picked up *Hussein*, also known as 'Saleem' at Berlin airport. 'e was on 'is way to another flight out of Germany. Trying to cover 'is tracks from France you see."

"What will happen to him?" asked Karl.

"That, I cannot divulge Monsieur. It is now a matter for the intelligence services."

"And the SD card?" I ventured, knowing the answer already.

"That will be take care of as well *Madame.*"

Evasive. Obviously we weren't going to privy to such highly sensitive information, despite what we'd been through. Probably better we didn't know anyway, I mused.

"And the intruder?" I paused looking at him and then Di quizzically. "There was an intruder?"

"Yes *Madame*. Though it may 'ave been one of my men that *Madame* 'arley was determined to shoot only a few nights ago." He smiled sardonically. "Once Saleem found out that *Madame* 'arley had the scarf 'e let 'is associate know and 'e attempted to enter the 'ouse this evening. We, of course were watching the house, waiting for someone to make a move. We knew that *Madame* 'arley life was threatened."

So the bait worked I thought grimly.

"And...you were able to catch him?" I of course, knew that answer. I recalled the black bag the men had put into the boot of the car just as we arrived.

He nodded staying quiet for a moment then said ambiguously.

"We 'ave dealt with 'im. Yes *Madame*."

We were all silent for a moment.

I looked at Di. She stared fixedly at a spot on the table, still looking thoroughly shattered. Looking how I felt. I noted she had sat silently, listening throughout. Not even a comment. These events had obviously taken their toll. I looked at my watch. It was after midnight.

"Come home with us Di. We can't leave you on your own tonight."

She shook her head pulling herself out of her thoughts.

"No, it's okay. Phil's on his way home." She saw my surprised look. "I spoke to him on the phone just before you came. His flight has been all arranged by *Monsieur...*" She looked at the man opposite hoping for an idea of a name.

"Let's say...*Pierre*" he said smiling. He was obviously trained to cope much better with the events of the past few days than we were.

"*Pierre*," Di repeated "has arranged for Phil to return sooner than expected. He should be here by morning. And to be honest, I just want to go to sleep. *Pierre*," she stressed his name "is staying overnight."

"As reassurance only, *Madame* 'arley" he looked at her kindly. "There is no further danger. They know we 'ave the information now. There is no further need for any of their operatives to be in France regarding this matter." He stood up suddenly. "Would you like help to the car *Madame* Patterson?"

So we were being dismissed. Karl responded.

"I can manage thank you, *Pierre*" he also stressed his name. *Pierre* shrugged as if the made up name idea was perhaps not as good an idea as he first thought.

Di saw us to the door and we hugged. Karl kissed her on the cheek.

"We'll meet up in a few days. When we've all rested. Come over for lunch."

"Of course." She waited until the car pulled away before closing the door. I rested my head against the back of the seat and looked out into the darkness. Despite the pain in my leg, I fell into a relaxed doze.

CHAPTER FIFTEEN

The next few days were spent in bed catching up on sleep and being fussed over by Karl. He reported on the visitors I'd had as they had the habit of turning up while I was asleep so he passed on their good wishes, even, I was astonished to hear, *Monsieur* Ferret. Karl, whose French was poorer than mine, managed to understand what he was saying because he said that *Monsieur* Ferret was trying very hard to speak much slower than babbling in his usual *patois*. I was touched by *Monsieur* Ferret's obvious concern and again resolved to make the extra effort to converse with him in future. Although sorry to have missed the well-wishers, I was glad to have avoided their questions. I really didn't want to dwell on the events of the past week and I had been told to keep most of it under wraps anyway.

The doctor arrived just before the weekend with a wooden crutch. The pain in my leg had begun to recede and he advised me to try walking a little each day using the crutch. I tried it out and found that I was rather a dab hand at using it. My leg grew stronger.

The Inspector came to inform Karl that he would not be continuing his investigations. We weren't sure how much information the Inspector had been privy to so simply accepted what he said and didn't provide him with any of our own thoughts about what had happened. However, we both got the distinct impression that the Inspector, having a suspicious nature, knew there was more to it than met the eye. He stated quite categorically that he'd been given orders from above to cease all further scrutiny and seemed as if he was expecting us to embellish him with more details. Because we didn't, Karl said he thought the Inspector was fairly miffed and we both thought he appeared downright hostile as he bade us farewell. I supposed it couldn't have been easy for him to have his power usurped and said I actually felt sorry for him.

We decided not to tell Aidan or Chloe anything about what had happened in the last week, knowing that they would only worry and there was nothing anyone could do about it now anyway. We spoke to them both over the following weeks and their lives were going on as usual.

Karl changed the complete lock on the hallway door. He said that he'd found a small piece of thin wire stuck inside it which was probably the reason it wasn't working. I assumed this was from whatever implement Saleem had used, in a crude attempt to open the door.

Aidan fixed the website and we found there was a backlog of emails, including one from Frederic, my gîte guest who had returned to Paris with his family early because of a reported burglary. He informed me that, although he was delighted his home was in one piece, he was quite perturbed to find that he had been the victim of a hoax call, as his home had not been burgled at all. He had tried to contact the policeman who had reported the burglary to him at the local *gendarmerie* but found they had no knowledge of his existence. What a surprise, I thought wryly.

To stem the flow of these constant reminders of past events, I focused all of my attention on the rest of the emails. Many requesting information about the dates available and facilities on site as well as around the area. I was delighted and spent most of my time, sitting on the terrace responding happily.

The weather was still unseasonably warm but there'd been a few showers, enough to keep the plants watered without needing extra from the water butt. Though not enough water to flood out Lesley's cellar. It meant she'd been able to get the concrete poured at last.

CHAPTER SIXTEEN

Karl invited everyone round for Sunday lunch, exactly two weeks to the day that I'd been left for dead. I was determined not to dwell on the past but simply enjoy the day. Karl announced he was going to make a proper English Sunday roast with Yorkshire puddings. He said he wasn't bothered about whether our French friends complained about the beef being overcooked. He wanted it to look cooked rather than still *mooing* as the French seemed to like it. His words not mine.

It was a little after midday and I was sitting at the table enjoying the weather and the view when everyone started to arrive.

Marie was the first. She relished these social occasions and turned up all bright eyed and bushy tailed. Quizzing me a little about what had happened I soon realised Karl had not told everyone the whole story. I, however, decided to stick to my guns and evaded her questions. I didn't want to think about it as it would spoil the day. To give her her due, Marie didn't persist but just left it alone. One day, I thought. Noticing she wasn't accompanied by her husband, I asked whether Jean would be arriving separately. She avoided my look and muttered something about him being too busy working. Again? I didn't pursue it.

When Sophie and André arrived I felt close to tears. I had not seen Sophie since the evening of the accident. We embraced warmly and she sat down next to me. Although she was wearing makeup there was still some obvious bruising around her chin and she walked rather stiffly. I assumed because she was still in some discomfort. Sensing that we needed a few minutes alone André feigned great interest in Karl's cooking and went off with him and Marie to the kitchen. To discuss the beef!

While they were gone Sophie told me it was the first time she had ventured out of André's house since returning with him from the hospital. On finding out that the brake cable on her car had been cut she had become very anxious and had been worried about getting into another car. Though not wanting to dwell on what had happened, I was still curious about her encounter with so called Mr Saleem. I still wondered how he had the impression that we knew more about him than we actually did. I also wondered about the missing time between her leaving Andrés house and the car accident.

She said that she began with a fairly convivial chat to Mr Saleem by the pool.

I interrupted "I thought he'd propositioned you, the way you looked when we nearly bumped into each other."

"No, no. Nothing like that. I introduced myself to him because of the Egyptian background you'd mentioned. I asked him, in Arabic, a few questions about where he was from. My father's family is from Giza which is a suburb of Cairo, so I wondered if he knew the area. He seemed evasive, saying that he hadn't been there for years because he had been living in Alexandria. I found that his accent, the way he pronounced certain words in Arabic, sounded as if he was more used to speaking Libyan Arabic. Libya, as you may know, borders Egypt. I made, what I thought at the time was an innocent remark about this. Little did I know that this was a little too close for comfort."

"Hindsight" I stated simply and shrugged.

"Yes" she agreed. After a pause she continued.

"So...by unintentionally discovering that he wasn't being truthful I'd made him become rather hostile. He changed the subject. Asked whether I thought I was dressed appropriately for a good Muslim.

I felt very angry. I told him I lived in a free country and could dress as I like. Religion had nothing to do with what I was wearing and anyway I was a Christian not Muslim. Having said my piece, I left. But all the while I was annoyed that I had risen to his bait. I think he only mentioned my clothing to deflect the attention away from himself." She paused.

"So when you saw me that evening you were going to tell me about the encounter?"

"No. I was going to tell you that I had contacted someone to find out if Mr Saleem was who he said he was. I wanted to do a little checking up on him. I have a reporter friend who works for Al Jazeera and who, as it happens, is Libyan. At the moment he is based in Paris. Because of the terrorist activity in France, he has been living there for several months to report on any terrorist situations that arise. Anyway, once he started digging around with the information and description I'd given him – it set off alarm bells and he had a *visit*." She looked at me conspiratorially.

"Oh" I returned the look. I assumed she meant the intelligence service.

"When I left that evening to go to André's, I didn't know any of this and did not for one moment suspect either of us was in danger".

"So the time between André's house and the crash...?" I began.

She nodded as I spoke. "Yes, I thought that must be a mystery to you...I had actually intended to stay at Andrés that night but around twelve thirty there was a visitor who made it very clear, that although he was not a threat, my life was in danger and I was to go with him to clear up some details of an enquiry they had ongoing into Mr Saleem. He seemed genuine and asked André to telephone the local police and speak to Inspector Maupetit to confirm that he indeed was genuine. Which he did. And he was. So how could I refuse? I needed to know more."

I was intrigued but hearing the voices in the kitchen willed Sophie to divulge the information quickly before the others came back to join us.

"I was asked to go alone to an address outside of the village...It was a little remote, to be honest, and in the dark...but apparently it was so that they could check no one had followed."

Seeing my look of horror she held up her hand. "Yes...yes...I know, André was horrified too but I had a good feeling, I didn't think that there was any risk...and that proved to be the case...Anyway, when I got there I met a man, I believe you know as *Pierre*?" She smiled wryly.

"Oh, yes..." The code word – *politician's cousin* came to mind.

"He showed me photographs of the man we knew as Mr Saleem and questioned me about him and his activities...not that I knew that much...and also the people I knew here. Of course, that included you and everything I knew about you. *Pierre* told me that Saleem was in France to retrieve something and would stop at nothing to get what he wanted. He swore me to secrecy saying that I mustn't let on that I knew he was dangerous or attempt to speak to Saleem about anything else. He told me to be on my guard and to keep our meeting secret. After leaving there, I stopped off at André's. I had to show him that I was safe even though I'd been told to keep quiet about the information I'd been given. But of course, I knew I could trust André. I explained that lives were at stake and that he must not *under any circumstances* tell anyone about the contact with the man I knew as Pierre. He agreed and insisted that I stay but I declined. I wanted to return here. For two reasons really. I needed to go through everything that had happened...get my head around it...what I'd learned. But also...in some way I needed to warn you without you knowing too much".

"So, if you'd stayed the night you probably would've been okay? "

She nodded. "If I hadn't *returned* to André's I would've been okay. I assume that's where the brake cable was cut."

I wondered if Mr Saleem or just, Saleem, as we now seemed to be calling him, in disgust, had cut the cable himself, or was it one of the others? Part of the cell. I didn't voice my thoughts.

"So since then you've been looked after by André"

Yes she said and he had been a wonderful carer. I wondered, knowing that Saleem was aware that she had survived the crash, how he hadn't made another attempt on her life. She explained.

"André's house was being watched. Armed men. Maybe they were spotted by Saleem and his men so they knew not to take the risk. I don't think anyone else...you know... neighbours and the like, were aware of anyone guarding it."

She also said that she no longer felt the need to warn me as she knew the intelligence service men were onto him and assumed they were secretly also guarding my house. She didn't think they'd allow Saleem to harm me. How wrong she was! Come to think of it, even the *stupid* code word, meant to be a help had actually been a hindrance. Overhearing Di and I talk about it might have been part of the reason Saleem made the decision to get rid of me!

"It doesn't seem to have been the case," she added ruefully.

"No – yet they seemed to be watching Di's house."

I thought back to the intruder. "But I think at that time – like the Inspector – they didn't know what Saleem was actually looking for...so they didn't know I had the information, which of course was in the scarf."

"Yes, you're probably right. Saleem knew you had the scarf somewhere but *Pierre* didn't know about it. He confessed to initially suspecting Di and Phil of being in on whatever Saleem was here for. He also couldn't work out why Saleem was staying as your guest. He surmised at first that it was so Saleem could liaise with Di without arousing suspicion. Then after you were found in the cellar, it was confirmation that Di was also in danger."

The others arrived back and took their seats around the table just as Sophie changed the subject and announced to everyone's surprise, except André's of course, that she was thinking of staying in France. I noticed André's frequent adoring glances toward Sophie during that afternoon. It was wonderful to see them so happy together.

Both Sophie and I were off the painkillers that day, so while Karl went back to the kitchen to check on the food, André and Marie played hosts by filling up the wine glasses. Lesley and Tim turned up a few minutes later. I joked that they must have been able to hear the wine being poured into the glasses. After the greetings they helped themselves to drinks and joined the rest of us at the table, chatting amiably about general day to day things. No reference to anything else, for which I was grateful.

Monsieur Lagard was the next to appear with news that *Monsieur* Ferret was visiting family so was unable to attend our little get together. For me, this was especially disappointing – keen as I was to thank him for the part he played in my rescue. I therefore made a mental note to visit him as soon as I was able, resolving to overcome the language barrier so that I could convey my heartfelt thanks.

Turning my attention to the group once again, I noticed *Monsieur* Lagard was as chirpy as ever, greeting everyone as if they were long lost friends. I watched him greet Sophie with such familiarity that it was as if she was already his daughter-in-law. He also, in all seriousness, offered me the use of his cane with the lion's head. He said I shouldn't be using a simple wooden stick because I'd been brave like a lion so should parade it proudly to reflect my courage. I was flattered and laughed at his sentiment, agreeing to use it for a few days. The reference to my courage made me wonder how much he actually knew.

Di and Phil were the last to arrive. I was glad that Di looked a lot more relaxed and rested, as if the last two weeks had washed away all memory of her ordeal. I soon realised that the events still occupied her mind when she embraced both me and Karl as if she wanted to never let us go.

About half an hour after everyone had arrived, Karl returned from the kitchen with a plate of *hors d'oeuvres*. Our guests responded cheerfully with laughter and cries of delight at the arrival of food. The jovial atmosphere and wine were taking effect. I took a moment to look around and reflect on how lucky we really were.

Dear Reader

If you enjoyed reading this story, I'd be very grateful if you would post a review, no matter how brief or lengthy, on amazon.com and/or amazon.co.uk.
I look forward to reading your comments!
Thank you so much.

GM Haley

NOTES ABOUT THE DEUX SEVRES REGION

Deux-Sèvres is a départment in the South West of France which literally means "two Sèvres": the Sèvre Nantaise and the Sèvre Niortaise are two rivers which have their sources in the department.

Deux-Sèvres was one of the 83 original départements created during the French Revolution on March 4, 1790.

The climate is mild, the annual temperature averaging 11 degrees Celsius.

The département remains rural. Wheat, oats, apples, and walnuts are the main products grow . The département is also well known for the breeding of cattle, mules, and horses. Dairy products such as goat's cheese are produced in significant quantities.

The south-west of the département, which includes the Marais Poitevin natural area and the Atlantic coast are major tourist attractions.

Niort, in the south of the département is the centre for growing vegetables and angelica. Vineyards are numerous in the north. With 60,000 inhabitants, Niort is an important commercial and administrative centre and capital. It is connected to Paris and Bordeaux by the A10 motorway.

The département has two railway stations on the TGV route between Paris and La Rochelle with a journey from Niort to Paris taking 2h15. It is also served by several TER Poitou-

Charentes regional railway routes, including a route from Poitiers via Niort to La Rochelle, a route from Niort to Saintes, and a route from Tours to Thouars and Bressuire.

A railway bus service operated as part of the TER Poitou-Charentes network follows the RN149 from Poitiers to Nantes, calling at Parthenay and Bressuire.

There is also an inter-urban bus service that connects the towns and villages of the département.

The nearest commercial airports are at Poitiers, La Rochelle and Nantes.

Printed in Poland
by Amazon Fulfillment
Poland Sp. z o.o., Wrocław

54513642R00143